Arthur James M. Bentley, Charles G. Griffinhoofe

Wintering in Egypt

Arthur James M. Bentley, Charles G. Griffinhoofe

Wintering in Egypt

ISBN/EAN: 9783337227937

Printed in Europe, USA, Canada, Australia, Japan

Cover: Foto ©Andreas Hilbeck / pixelio.de

More available books at **www.hansebooks.com**

WINTERING IN EGYPT.

BY

ARTHUR J. M. BENTLEY, M.D.,

AND

REV. C. G. GRIFFINHOOFE, M.A.

PART I.

UNDER THE SHADOW OF THE PYRAMIDS.

PART II.

HINTS TO INVALIDS.

LONDON:

SIMPKIN, MARSHALL, HAMILTON, KENT & Co. Ltd.

1894.

PREFACE.

THE amateur who, after a brief visit to a land which other people do understand though he does not, ventures to give forth to the world a statement treating of the country in general, and to advance opinions as to what seem to him to be needed reforms, gains for himself well merited condemnation. In writing these pages we have therefore kept before us, as far as possible, our original intention to notice only one particular part of Egypt, a limited area about which our long residence on the spot had given us some right to speak.

Our endeavour has been to throw light on an enjoyable way of spending the winter, and to record our experiences in a part of the world which is full of unique interest.

In so far as we have mentioned the manners and customs of the Arabs, we have expressed opinions with which we believe English residents in the country agree.

We submit, therefore, these pages to the public trusting that they may go some way towards enlivening the days of those whose lot it is to ' winter in Egypt.'

LONDON,   A. J. M. B.
November, 1894   C. G. G.

Contents.

Illustrations.

PART I.

UNDER THE SHADOW OF THE PYRAMIDS,

BY

ARTHUR J. M. BENTLEY, M.D.

PHYSICIAN TO MENA HOUSE, CAIRO ; EMERITUS PRESIDENT ROYAL MEDICAL
SOCIETY, EDIN. ; FORMERLY COLONIAL SURGEON STRAITS SETTLEMENTS,
MEDICAL ADVISER TO THE JOHORE GOVERNMENT, AND PHYSICIAN
TO H.H. THE SULTAN.

AND

C. G. GRIFFINHOOFE, M.A.

LATE SENIOR CURATE OF ST. ANDREW'S, WELLS STREET ; AND
SOMETIME CHAPLAIN OF MENA.

LONDON :

SIMPKIN, MARSHALL, HAMILTON, KENT & Co. Ltd.

1894.

CHAPTER I.

WHEN the actual day for leaving England comes, travellers generally find that, with all its faults, they love the country still—no better place could be, if only its position on the globe did not necessitate in winter such joyless weather.

No one could look very cheerful on the November morning on which we sailed. The clouds were of the dullest leaden hue ; only a little wind was blowing, but that was cold ; London was wrapt in a damp fog, and the dreariness of the docks was appalling ; so gloomy did everything look that we were not sorry when the vessel started and the last farewells were over.

The first meal on board is a somewhat stiff affair ; no one knows his neighbour, and the motion of the ship is unpleasant to constitutions which have not yet become accustomed to the roll. The best way is to go early to sleep ; in the morning things begin to look " ship-shape " ; there is no going back, and therefore the inevitable must be accepted ; but there are sad hearts on board, and well there may be, for partings are trying events.

The view at sea is somewhat disappointing and decidedly monotonous, and the proof of this is the joy with which even distant land or a passing boat is hailed. There is a sense of horror, too, about the great deep on a dark night when neither moon nor stars are visible, and as we lean over the bulwarks, all that can be seen is the foam made by the screw and . the crests of the angry waves. We have thought sometimes in the silence of that loneliness, when the deck has been deserted by all the passengers, how awful it would be if by any accident we stumbled overboard, and how appalling would be the death in those black engulfing waves, while all who could have helped were being borne rapidly away.

We were hardly forty hours from London, and already the sky was gloriously bright, and we could feel the sun ; overcoats were left off, and we experienced a sense of composure, for we knew that for one winter at least the cold was past.

We had always heard much of the waves of the Atlantic—great and swelling they certainly are. Compared with that of the Mediterranean sea, the roll of the Atlantic is big ; but the Bay of Biscay, when we crossed, was fairly calm, and it seemed to us that there was more to fear off the coast of Portugal, where the swell rolls back from those great rugged perpendicular frowning cliffs, near to which vessels pass.

Within four and a half days from home we were anchored at Gibraltar under that huge rock which appears to have grown there by mistake. We were glad to stretch our legs, and walk through the town, which seems to be the home of shot and shell. The place bristled with forts and "Tommy Atkins" in all his glory was in evidence at every turn, while cannon mouths obtruded at corners of the gardens. A regiment of the Queen was at drill; the pride in our English birth rose up, as well it might; and we wondered whether we shall ever be foolish enough, as a nation, to let the fortress pass from us.

We turned our steps to the town, and were delighted with the shops—pottery of capital design can be got here in plenty, and we thought how much it would be prized in London—gaily painted and fringed tambourines took our fancy, though we are not " Salvation army " admirers; but in the market we found to our disgust that the majority of things to be sold were cheap vulgar Birmingham goods. Strangers of every land are to be met in " Gib," and the Moors cut a striking figure in their sack-like cloaks with pointed hoods.

We were sorry to leave the gay bright town, but it was time to rejoin our boat.

During more days of calm and sunny weather we saw sights about which we had often heard; —a shoal of porpoises—a turtle—a shark—a spouting whale, and a flying fish all disported themselves for our special benefit. The colour of the sea had uniformly been a deep purple indigo; the phosphorescence, too, at night was beautiful, and we had the satisfaction of feeling, we were rapidly making way. A few hours more, and we were at Naples. Boats of all kinds surrounded us, propelled by the handsome light-hearted rowers; on every side was the twanging of mandolines, accompanied by the rich Italian voice. " Funiculi funicula " and " Margherita " were the songs which everyone sang.

We passed our day in the town and at the Museum ; the time allowed on shore admits on some occasions of a visit to Pompeii. Vendors of all kinds of goods were on board towards the hour of departure; we noticed that the prices fell prodigiously, as the time available for bargaining grew less. It was dark when we left that lovely bay, and a crack in the side of Vesuvius showed the angry glow of subterraneous fire. Stromboli, with its smoking crater and houses dotted on the green below, struck us as an uncomfortable place in which to live ; but the passage through the Straits of Messina left a charming impression on our minds.

CHAPTER II.

SOMETHING seemed to tell us we were nearing Alexandria, and a look shorewards revealed to us the fact that land was close by. The first sight of the coast is disappointing—nothing more than a dull stretch of sand, with ruins of silent forts. To the left shines out in a wealth of splendour the Palace of Ras-et-Tin. Steam was actually being slowed down, and we were passing between vessels of many nations—a little more, and we were in port.

What a sight it was! A sea of perfectly transparent blue, rippling in gorgeous sunlight. Before us was an Eastern town, and the houses were actually white. It is curious, after some months stay under that brilliant sky, to find on arrival at what are known as sunny parts of Europe—Sicily, for instance —how the glory of brightness seems gone. The sunlight of Egypt is to that of Europe as electric light to ordinary gas.

A swaying crowd was waiting to board us. Every-one was shouting and gesticulating, and the noise was terrific. There was colour everywhere; and a con-tinuous procession of turbaned heads of men in "smocks" of light or dark blue; stately old men wearing the black abayeh, very much like a college gown ; boys with various coloured waistcoats, and cloths of many hues round their necks and heads ; officers in handsome uniforms ; Cook's men in scarlet jerseys with large yellow letters ;—a sight of joy to tourists, for in our travels we have found Cook's officials invaluable.

The porters have a strange facility for carrying heavy baggage in the east. The package is supported on the back, and kept there by the hands placed underneath. We have seen Arabs thus carry cumbersome weights at which an Englishman would rebel. Arrived at the destination, they simply sit down backwards on the ground-—they seem none the worse, and the box is standing on end unharmed.

At last we were on shore and our luggage was borne off to the customs, and quickly passed. A carriage whirled us through the town to Abbat's hotel past lovely gardens, where pointzettias as large as lilac shrubs were in full and luxuriant bloom with what look like flowers of a foot or more in diameter at least. The garden of Abbat's hotel is always delightful: all round it are yellow walls, relieved, however, by the charming green of the shutters ; on one side is a kind of cloister of the same arrangement ; running across the garden is a small bridge, and as a means of reaching this from below there is a spiral staircase of very pretty design with an umbrella-like top ; two stone lions survey the scene of peace : lovely palms sway gently in the breeze ; many birds chirp and hop in pretty cages, and over all the Egyptian sun diffuses its delightful warmth.

After a rest we went forth to see the wonders

of the town. It was strange to feel we were in what was formerly one of the greatest cities of the world. Under the Ptolemies Alexandria rose to eminence. It was here that Euclid the great geometrician lived; here also was once the noted lighthouse and the far-famed library, a great part of the books of which were used to light bath fires, because, forsooth, they were other than the Koran. Here the Septuagint Greek Version of the Jewish Scriptures was made, which prepared the way largely for the knowledge of the Jewish religion and the coming of the Christ. From Alexandria the sainted body of Mark the Evangelist was shipped to lovely Venice. Apollos and Jerome, Athanasius and Antony, Cyril and even Cleopatra were all connected in history with this city. Later on it has been famous for the massacre of Europeans in 1882, and the subsequent bombardment.

One thing we did was to view the large Greek church close by. Bells clanging as if to wake the dead had warned us it was somewhere at hand and we tried the doors. An Arab proffered his aid, but we refused; like a leech he stuck to us, however; at last we were obliged to let him gain the admission which we had not achieved, and a grin of conscious triumph crossed his swarthy face. And here let us remark an Arab who is determined to be your guide will generally conquer in the end; he knows the ropes better than you, and as very often submit you must, it is better to submit pleasantly and at once. Inside the building we found an absence of anything tawdry. The church like others in the East possesses a highly

B

decorated screen ; behind this we passed and found
a by no means unusual mixture of neatness and
incongruous surroundings. The altar was richly clad,
and on it lay the Book of the Holy Gospels covered
with a beautiful veil ; by the side of this was a very
dirty prayer-book and a small jar containing incense;
the lid had on it in English characters the name of a
tooth-paste firm.

We then turned our steps to the town and witnessed
as we passed an amusing fight between two boys, an
interested crowd of brother shoeblacks meanwhile
looking on. The combatants evinced no very great
display of temper, and they rather mauled than hit each
other. They were far less keen than London street
arabs would have been, for they quite forgot to keep
any look out for the officers of the law ; a policeman
leisurely approached, gave each a whack, and led both
off to prison. All their anger seemed to have vanished
and they were dreamily led away, taking it all as a
part of the day's business.

The time was up for us to leave for Cairo. At the
station we found a scene of confusion ; nothing was
known, nothing was in order ; it was quite a labour
to purchase cigarrettes and to get the proper change
given, for the platform was crowded with touts and
guides who made a true Eastern turmoil. After
half an hour we got off. The view as we passed
along was novel and interesting. The general impression was of sand diversified with the grey green palms
and fields of cotton, mud villages with white-washed
mosques and quaint Arab cemeteries, rough and
primitive in the extreme. Horses seemed to have

given place to camels and donkeys, and we remarked how well the ugly appearance of the former fitted in with the surroundings.

Groups of striking figures were returning from work along the odd looking roads, birds of many kinds seemed to abound, some were specially graceful, which are commonly called the white ibises, or paddy birds, but are really a kind of heron—later on we will say more about them. The scene at the stations *en route* is always engrossing and we learned that the aim of an Arab's life seems to be to get paid for doing nothing. A ceaseless demand is made for backsheesh ; sometimes it is asked for in return for answering a question or for being a nuisance. This habit of craving for money just because you have more than they is bad, and a great blot upon the character of the Egyptians. We may well be thankful that to a great extent Englishmen can claim immunity from a similar fault : though we remember hearing once how in college days a friend had saved a lad from drowning, and was somewhat surprised on the following morning to receive a visit from the boy's father asking for money to drink the health of the man who had saved his child's life.

The stolid ease and self-satisfaction of the rich and well-to-do was in striking contrast with the down-trodden look of those who were evidently poor. The injustice and cruel oppression which the lower classes for years endured cannot be forgotten all at once. Things are better now, but we have often seen Arabs when they felt they were being treated unfairly put on the most piteous look of consciousness that for them justice was not to be. Why some of them should be so poor in a land where life is so easily and so cheaply sustained by a diet of tomatoes and bread and lentils is not for us to say,* but very poor many of them are, and their poverty has often made us sad. We remember once seeing a resident at Mena, one of the kindest and most generous of men, give a substantial coin to a poor old blind man who was sunning himself by the side of the mud hovel which he dignified by the name of home. The old fellow was mainly supported by his son, the ugliest and "eeriest" boy we ever remember seeing. His joy at the gift was a sight to see : he promptly hugged the coin in his hand and spat upon it for luck, sorrowing that his poor blind eyes could no longer look upon its form. God reward you ! was the old Muslim's simple prayer. We trust the wish may come true.

The train had quickly sped, and we were at Cairo. Porters and dragomans from the various hotels were there in numbers, and the same scene of turmoil to a certain extent had to be gone through. By all means have your decision clearly made before arrival as to which hotel you mean to patronize—firmness on this point is needed. We hailed a man wearing the neat and attractive uniform of Mena House, and all our troubles were at an end. We remember once at this station experiencing great courtesy during a difficulty from a young English commissioned officer of the

---

* An Arab once told us that food and tobacco cost him one piastre (2½d.) a day. A field labourer usually receives as wages about three piastres (7½d.) a day.

BOATS ON THE NILE.

By permission, from a photograph by Zangaki.

Egyptian police ; politeness goes far : for though we were never able to find out his name, his charming manner we have not forgotten. The luggage was placed on a mule-cart, and we entered a victoria to be taken to the Pyramids.

Everywhere colour abounded : passing over the Nile Bridge we admired the broad stretch of river on which by day scud the many boats with their graceful wing-like sails. The scent of the orange-blossoms made us rejoice as we reached the lovely Gizeh gardens. We were now in the avenue of lebbek trees,* seven miles in length, which stretches right to Mena. By the command of a late Khedive " this highway in the desert was made straight " in a brief space of time. Gradually the Pyramids seemed to grow in size ; they looked near when we started, presently they seemed to be at hand. Viewed from this road at the hour of sunset they assume a purple tinge, while the sky behind is ablaze with gold and scarlet and even the very water at the side of the way seems lit up and to take the colour of blood.

We can never efface from our memory our first experience of this drive. We had arrived at Cairo late, and a gorgeously dressed personage had taken us under his charge. We had not been unused to high official life in England, but the dignified bearing of this man with his long robes of gold and white surmounted by a burnous of similar embroidered work, together with a silk handkerchief of brilliant colouring round his head, made us really think him an Arch-bishop at least   He proved afterwards to our chagrin

---

* Albizzia Lebbek.

to be only a dragoman, and willing to accept
even small backsheesh. The moon was shining in
all its glory and the scene was solemn as we
drove to the hotel. Our arrival thus late was only
welcomed at first by the night watchman : soon
however lights began to flicker from stables and
huts ; stately Arab forms made their salaam ; it
seemed so strange in the stillness of midnight to be
in this land of wonders, beneath the shadow of those
huge tombs hoary with a venerable antiquity, about
which we had so often heard—

> Before us rose in wonderful array,
> Those works where man has rivalled nature most
> Those Pyramids, that fear no more decay
> Than waves inflict upon the rockiest coast,
> Or winds on mountain-steeps, and like endurance boast.*

Our swarthy guides led us through the verandah to
the front door of the hotel and sounded both electric
bells, night and day ; we strongly recommend this
practice, for it quickly brought the porter only
half dressed, complaining that we seemed somewhat
impatient ; he let us in and we found ourselves in a
palatial hall where Moorish architecture and furniture
blended in exquisite accord. We learned next day that
our arrival had not been hailed with pleasure by the rest
of the visitors, whom the clanging of the electric bells
seemed almost universally to have aroused from sleep.
We, however, were not to blame ; our coming so late
was an unusual event. Our journey was at an end,
and we retired to rest with our windows open,
remembering that we had left England in snow.

* *Burden of Egypt.* Lord Houghton.

CHAPTER III.

THE neighbourhood of the Pyramids is one of the most interesting spots in the world. A strange sense of mystery creeps over the mind of the Englishman as he gazes on those stupendous monuments of a partially understood and long distant past, while over him looms that glorious blue sky flooded with radiant light. On one side lies the trackless, weird, apparently unending, desert, with its ever-changing light and shade; undulating like the storm-tossed Atlantic; crossed by numberless sierra-like ridges of hills, which rise at times to considerable height, and then as suddenly cease; streaked everywhere with rock-dotted valleys; possessing a sparse, starved vegetation of its own which near any shaded spot blossoms out into a tiny attempt at stronger growth; gleaming at times like old gold when the sun illumines the dry clean sand; shadowed again with exquisite purple when the light throws the curious pale blue rocks into relief; at times gladdening the heart with its joyous brightness and peace; at times deeply impressive by its sombre, sober-minded expression of vastness, monotony, and desolation. Stretching far and wide for thousands of miles beyond the ken of human eye, many a land of interest borders on this self-same extensive desert.

Tripoli and Algeria and Morocco, Sierra Leone and Ashantee, Abyssinia, and Khartum—all these places touch the desert on which we gaze ; for it forms the heart of mighty Africa, which partly unexplored and uninhabited and virtually unknown still remains the sealed country of the Equator.

On the other side lies the Nile valley, the fertile tract of land, all length, and no breadth, which stretches from the Mediterranean to the very heart of Africa, bearing in its soft green bed the historic mysterious river, which with varying conditions ceaselessly flows from Victoria Nyanza to the sea, some 3,000 miles. The plain owes all its fertility to the overflowing waters which year by year deposit their muddy residuum over its whole surface, and then quietly, soberly, and unobtrusively withdraw.   Before us is nothing but the brilliant green of growing corn, green which must be seen to be realized : at times in the distance streaked with a line of vivid yellow where a field of mustard crosses the scene.   Villages of mud-built houses dot the plain, and palm groves lend beauty to the landscape.   The vast flat valley is given up to agriculture, and repays to the hundredfold the small amount of labour that it needs.

Not far away once stood Memphis, the capital of lower Egypt, then a city of renown, rejoicing in lovely buildings and gardens, and interesting to a degree : but represented now only by its ruins.

Farther to the north, by the winding river, lies the city that does duty as the modern capital of Egypt— an eastern city with a western fringe, which borders but does not materially alter the more ancient

garment : a city which like the phœnix has risen from
the ruins of more glorious predecessors. Memphis,
and Fostat, and Babylon live again in Cairo of
to-day. As we gaze, two things stand distinctly
out in the strong clear light, though they are ten
miles away ;—the minarets of the citadel mosque, and
the Mokattam range of hills behind ; but these things
are by the way. What does seem of surpassing
interest to all who dwell at Mena is the enormous
cemetery of ages long past, which stretches for miles
along the desert edge, and is crowned by the great
pyramids. It is one great waste of rock-strewn sand
interspersed with countless sepulchres, some of which
have been rifled, desecrated, and robbed, and most of
them at some time explored.

CHAPTER IV.

MENA HOUSE.

MENA House is a group of buildings which have
grown by degrees. An Englishman is said once to
have passed a winter in this neighbourhood long
before the hotel was thought of, and finding the climate
very beneficial to his form of lung complaint,
determined that others should be led to know of the
invigorating character of the air. Hence was built
the first part of the hotel, quite a small house. From
that it has grown to its present size.

A full and an illustrated description of the
various rooms and arrangements can be found in a
book which the hotel provides. We only single out
here one or two particulars of interest as worthy of
special mention. The exercise of perfect taste and
artistic refinement have brought it about that the
appearance of the interior of Mena is gratifying in
the extreme. Much trouble was taken to provide the
lovely specimens of mooshrabeah work—that special
trade of the country in ornamental wood which everywhere abounds through the house in the form of
mantlepieces and mirror frames, window screens and
balconies, corridors and doorways ; even the Arab
museum in Cairo has hardly more representative
examples of it ; in odd, out of the way corners

MENA HOUSE, PYRAMIDS, CAIRO.

splendid specimens exist, and the use thus made of it gives to the whole building a correct Egyptian tone. There are also several panels of inlaid coloured marbles worked in that style alone allowable to Muslims, who were forbidden to make a likeness of any living form, of the blending and intersection of squares and circles, and straight lines and curves in endless combination. This kind of art is prevalent in every mosque. It certainly has much to recommend it, and draws out the full ingenuity of the designer.*

The dining hall is a good example of work after the Moorish style ; for the excellence of its construction the architect deserves every credit. The adaptation of ancient rules to modern needs has met with striking success.

The chapel is the last of the buildings erected. Externally it is not beautiful, but inside the appearance is all that could be wished. In a Muslim land, where nothing ecclesiastical can be obtained, and where all sense of what is fitting is absent from an Arab's breast, the task of arranging for a satisfactory church is much increased in difficulty. As a rule the Mohammedans care little for the building, though one Arab we knew displayed great interest in its decoration. Notwithstanding, therefore, that from native sources little help was forthcoming, the many costly benefactions, memorials, and gifts of Mena

---

* For those who are interested in *patterns*, we recommend the study of the marks left in the sand by the movement of the small scarab beetle an insect which everywhere abounds.

visitors have given to the building an appearance which makes it fit for the reverent worship of the English Church.*

It is pleasant as one passes through the garden of "the precincts" to smell the delightful fragrance of the mignonette which even in the depth of winter is in full bloom. There are many other buildings at Mena which are worth seeing. The swimming bath and the dark photographing room are perhaps the most useful of these.

There are arrangements for tennis, croquet, archery and golf; while opportunities for riding and driving exist on every side. We joined one season in reviving the game of golf beside the Pyramids, on links which are by no means bad. A friend who was always ready for a joke used to assure the novices in the art of the game that it was useless to try and play without a bulger; application was accordingly made by one enthusiast at the shop adjoining the hotel for the club in question. The Indian in charge at first seemed staggered at the request. "What for you want vulture?" he asked. Explanations ensued, and he vouchsafed the reply, "in my shop plenty drivers, plenty cleeks, but I no have *bulliger*."

But the real charm of the place lies in its atmosphere, which seems to be composed of sunlight, and dryness, and warmth. People ask sometimes what there is to do at Mena. We reply the

---

* A correspondent in "The Guardian," August 29th, 1894, speaking of Bishop Blyth's Visitation Tour, makes mention of "the pretty chapel of Mena House, full of gifts and memorials."

THE DINING HALL, MENA HOUSE.

C

living in such a climate is in itself a joy, and the mere basking in the sun takes up a lot of time. In a land of perpetual sunshine it is wonderful how the willingness to do nothing grows upon human beings, who at other times to be happy must be continually employed. There are always things to interest the mind. Scenes of graceful grouping of colour are ever before the eye. The sunsets and, what is more, the afterglow, must be seen to be believed. Groups of natives make perfect pictures for the camera, for which in Egypt there is a wide field of scope.

CHAPTER V.

INSIDE THE GREAT PYRAMID.

THE great interest of Mena is its close proximity to the larger Pyramids, to the so-called Temple of the Sphinx, and to the Sphinx itself. In addition to these, the sight-seeing in and around Cairo may conveniently be done from Mena, while excursions can also easily be made to the site of Memphis, to Aboo-roash, and to Sakkarah, and even to the Petrified Forest.

A full description of the Temple of the Sphinx may be found in any guide-book. Opinions differ as to its antiquity, but the balance of testimony, perhaps points to its being the most ancient structure on the spot. Probably it is one of the very oldest of the temples of the world ; the marvellous massiveness, and the absence of inscriptions, may go some way to give this theory support. Whether it was originally a temple proper, or a tomb, is a matter of dispute. Where great men differ, it is not for us to decide, but a tomb in some respects it probably was. The awkward irregular slanting entrance fits in very badly with the accurately squared sides of the temple, and the oddly cut well is possibly of later date.

In drawing attention to a few special points, we may notice that the curiously arranged sockets for the vanished folding doors, which are drilled in the huge granite masses which form the walls, are cut very smoothly, as if by a diamond drill ; yet cut in a place so difficult to reach that it seems almost impossible to conceive how the work was done.

Some of the blocks of granite are of enormous size. One is nearly 20 ft. by 5 ft., and of proportionate thickness. Huge blocks of alabaster may be also found in some of the chambers. The marks on the floor of the temple proper have been thought by some to indicate that statues once stood here. We should, too, like to know how and why on one side and on only one, have such large pieces been chipped away from those blocks, which form a kind of roof to the columns.

A view of the temple, which is instructive, can be gained from the sand hill at the side, where one learns how the original constructors, first of all, cut right down into the solid rock, making various chambers, and then faced the whole hollowed-out space with those massive granite walls.

We shall not, as we have said, attempt to describe the Sphinx—that has often enough been done—all we say is that we have seen it under many conditions in the broad glare of day, and at night ; but the time when, to our minds, it looked most mysterious, was at an early hour on a December evening, just before the full moon.* The day gradually died, and in front of the Sphinx the moon rose : we have never our-

* We mention this, in order that many who are not allowed to go up at night to view the monument, may still see it under striking circum-stances.

selves been quite able to rise to the full height of
imagination, and to find all the mystery and impres-
siveness which some read into a rather common-place
countenance, but that there are many minds who are
thus impressed, we freely admit; certainly, in the
half light which then partly hid its blemishes, there
was something very striking in that stolid look of the
face so sharply cut out of the natural rock.

It is well to remember that the figure is that of a
lion with a man's head, the beard of which can be
seen in the British Museum. The height of the
whole figure is much greater than is imagined. We
watched one day a full-grown Arab scaling the side
to reach the top: as he came down, we saw that
his height (which we will call 6 ft.) was almost the
length of the Sphinx's *ear*. The remains of the red
colour which once brightened the somewhat stern
features, may still be clearly seen.

The ascent, and still more the descent of the Great
Pyramid, is liable to produce giddiness in some people,
and we have sometimes feared that if we mounted to
the top, we should have to stay there for good, like
S. Simeon Stylites on his column. Those who
have reached the top—and the bottom—in safety,
and they are many, are of opinion that the *general*
view from the summit is not better than that which
can be obtained from the Citadel, but that the actual
survey of the way in which the ancient cemetery
immediately around was laid out, is highly instructive,
and can alone be understood when seen from that
position.

We did once penetrate inside, and when we reached

the hotel, and all was over, we felt indeed proud of our achievement ; but we determined never to repeat it. For those who intend to make the entry, let us recommend the wearing of tennis-shoes and light coloured clothes, for the experience is a dusty one. As regards the selection of time, we advise an hour before dinner, whereby an adjournment can be made from the expedition to a bath.

The fact that we were well known at Mena secured for us, when we did definitely announce our intention of achieving the entrance or perishing in the attempt, the promise of two great concessions on the part of the Bedouin guides—first, that we should pay no more than was legitimately due for services rendered, and secondly, that we should not be accompanied by more Arabs than necessary.

We set out on the evening of Boxing Day, and could not help thinking how differently our friends were engaged in England. The afternoon had been warm, and twilight was now gathering round. The party was a pleasant one, and consisted of a kindly natured old English gentleman, who had rather an aversion to climbing, and a very decided one to being hurried and pushed ; a Harrow boy, to whom steps and slippery passages seemed a natural hunting ground, and who always got everywhere first ; two other friends, who required a good deal of "lifting," and occasionally "blocked the way"; ourselves, and the Arabs who after all were there in full force : for come they would, and come they did in larger numbers than we needed.

From the corner of the Pyramid the ascent is

begun over steps and rubbish heaps to the actual entrance, which is in the north face, some distance above the ground. This in itself is a giddy piece of work, but we soon found a ledge on which to rest ·before going in. Then begins a descent of some 50 feet down a slippery square passage, too low for standing in, which leads like a rabbit hole into the interior. At the bottom of this we had to stoop, and crawl under a portcullis of granite, only 3 ft. high. Once through this, we found ourselves in an uneven chamber of rock, in one side of which steps had been cut; up these, for about 10 ft., we had to climb, and then by clambering on to a ledge, we found ourselves in the gallery that led upwards. After a crawl of some distance over · polished granite which is so slippery that if we once slid back, we felt we should not stop till we reached the bottom, we arrived at a level space. Again the ascent begins, but for some distance the centre of the sloping pavement of the gallery is cut away to admit of an entrance to another corridor below, and in place of the broad footway, only ledges at the side remain. Up these narrow shelves tourists must crawl clinging tight to the wall; or else avail themselves of holes cut in the sides, while standing in mid-air with legs far apart, and a yawning hollow beneath. Once past this, the gap in the footway ceases, and except for the slippery character of the stone, the climb is easy. In the King's Chamber there is little to see, but the impression of awe struck us, and we realised that we were in the centre of a mountain of stones laid by human hands.

If the ascent is fairly easy, certainly the descent is the harder of the two, and when coming down, we reached the yawning gap with only a shelf on each side down which to crawl, and a good fall below us if we slipped—we wondered why here, where so many pass, the idea of making some wooden steps had never entered Arab heads ; until such steps are placed there, the going into the Pyramid can never be other than an awkward climb for ladies, and a not altogether pleasant one for men. We were thankful to get into the open air, and to feel "we had done it." The impression left on our minds is a confused medley of many things—air that seemed to have been stagnant for centuries ; dust that pervaded all things ; candles which dropped their grease over clothes and hands ; shining faces and flashing eyes of Arabs ; long galleries of polished granite, which gleamed and looked mysterious in the fitful candle-light ; strong arms and hands of guides, who certainly proved themselves invaluable ; chattering voices which made a horrid din, and echoed and re-echoed in the long tunnels ; scents, partly of spices and partly of measureless antiquity—and over all these the sense of heat which, though by no means unbearable, was very perceptible ; and of a great enwrapping horror of darkness which the candles only seemed to make more intense.

We had been inside "the biggest " thing in tombs in the world, wonderful in its perfect construction and awful massiveness ; for six or seven thousand years that great mountain has probably been standing. Long before Abraham moved from Ur of

the Chaldees, this structure was already old.   Possibly,
when it was built, the Sphinx was already carved, and
the Temple of the Sphinx may even stretch into the still
more dim and distant past.   What will have happened
in another 6,000 years to those marvels of stone ?

> Virtue alone outbuilds the Pyramids,
> Her monuments shall last when Egypt's fall. *

* Young's *Night Thoughts*.

CHAPTER VI.

THE CEMETERY OF MEMPHIS.

FOR nearly twenty miles along the desert edge, there is one vast cemetery. From Aboo-roash past Gizeh and Sakkarah it stretches to Dashoor and Mêdum. No one knows all that lies beneath. Much indeed has been discovered and overhauled, but the continual drifting of the sand effectually covers every thing and has done so for centuries gone by. Without permission of the authorities digging is not allowed, but the stirring of the sand may at any time bring some small treasure to light. Of one thing we may be sure, the Arabs know a great deal; if there is anything valuable to be found they are more or less acquainted with the spot; if they let strangers search in peace it is because there is nothing to be obtained. Still there is always the chance of picking something up. Men are but mortal, and robbers of tombs may sometimes drop odds and ends of booty which a European would greatly prize. We have picked up small atoms of interest, although of no value; but their valuelessness is to some extent compensated by the charm of search.

The exploration of any part of that long table land of graves is full of interest.

There are pyramids which look as if they had never

been finished, massive in their solid ugliness, surrounded
by rubbish-heaps of stone, and duly set according to
the compass, and each possessing on one side a ruined
temple, or something that does duty for one, where
the ancient rites were performed ; pyramids great,
which in the fading sunlight look like solid gold, and
pyramids small ; pyramids which have nobly stood
the wear and tear of ages, and pyramids of which
the shape is nearly wholly gone; less important tombs
called mastabas, large rambling places which are divided
into chambers adorned with painting and sculptured
figures and endless hieroglyphs and ornamented
recesses, and subdivided into rooms where on entering
you experience a fearful sense of oppressive air, and
where you bend down in passages until you think your
back is broken and realise at last the only way is to
crawl.

There are also rock-hewn caverns with marks of
smoke where the natives lit their fires when they used
them as dwelling houses ; caverns that are large, and
containing perhaps half-a-dozen rooms all cut out of
the solid rock and beautified only by decapitated
heroes and gods whose shape is gone ; caverns with
wooden doors and inhabited even now; and caverns that
are only the abode of snakes and bats.   There are
great gaping four-sided burial shafts down which it
makes you shudder to look, while a stone seems to
take a minute to reach the bottom; shafts too numerous
to count which pierce into the very bowels of the earth,
down which in the old days the mummies were let by
ropes but which are now only nesting places for owls
and other birds ; tombs with carved lintels, oddly

VIEW OF THE GREAT PYRAMID FROM THE SWIMMING BATH, MENA HOUSE.

placed and now all plundered and desecrated and only redolent with the odour of the dust of years.

Inside or outside these tombs may be found fragments of many bones, sculls of dark coffee colour with their well-set grinning teeth still intact, pieces of little blue images with which the soul of the dead was supposed to find companionship, bits of resinous pitch that will melt after all these thousands of years, scraps of mummy cloth soaked in natron, bits of coffins and atoms of necklet charms ; everywhere is interest, but it is the interest of a charnel-house, for the whole place is strewn with bones. The scene is diversified with marks of wild beasts in the sand—jackal and lynx and fox and an occasional hyena.

Anyone capable of walking will find his afternoon made pleasant by the few following hints about matters of interest outside the general run. At the base of the front of the great Pyramid may still be seen in the original position two of the huge surface stones. So carefully are they cut and cemented that not even a penknife will penetrate the section—so exactly was every stone planned. At the corner of the north-west angle is the iron ring marking the limit to which the angle line extended.* Passing on to the corresponding space before the second Pyramid we see those strange tables of rock on which it is said the stones were wrought. Above in the face of the surrounding wall are some hieroglyphs splendidly cut. As we continue to pass round there are caverns with roofs cut in the

---

* The space occupied by the base of the Great Pyramid is said to be about the size of Lincoln's Inn Fields in London.

likeness of tree trunks.   Some way to the south-east
of this pyramid there may be found a square of
ground bounded by natural rock, in one corner of
which is a typical tomb.   The entrance is down steps
under a carved lintel ; inside, the place is full of interest
for the tomb is old, and the spot has been made ad-
ditionally sacred by the recent burial of a shêkh.
When we entered our guide seemed terribly alarmed :
for a long time he refused to come in, and only did
so after saying some prayers with intense devotion.
We remember an interesting incident one Sunday
afternoon with reference to this particular tomb which
was then unknown to us.   We walked in this direction ; the day was sweetly peaceful—not peaceful like
an English Sunday which has a charm all its
own, but still a day when all was calm ; our conversation had for some time flagged : even the one
of us most given to making jokes seemed impressed
by the occasion and was silent.   All around there was
a deathly stillness—the sunlight slept upon the sand—
not even a bird soared overhead—all was still—suddenly from the heart of the rock came a weird sad
sound as of a man in woe.   The wail was continued
in strange sorrowful modulation in some ways like a
Gregorian chant.*

We learned afterwards it was a dervish singing
within this tomb, which he made his home, verses of

---

* A Bishop who shall be nameless once told us there was nothing
new to him in plainsong tones : for in the heart of Africa he had
known them as the attempts at song of the native tribes.   Certainly
around Mena those who care for Gregorian chants can hear, if they
keep their ears open, enough and to spare.

the Koran in that minor key of which they are so fond.
The voice was not unmusical, but it sounded uncanny
in the extreme. We listened for awhile and then
moved nearer; the chanting ceased; the holy man
had heard our steps, and his communing with his soul
for the time was stopped, and once more stillness
reigned around. It was as if we had listened to some
anthem of a bygone age that reached us from the
heart of the earth, and it will be years before the
strange effect produced fades from our mind.

Not far away may be found Campbell's tomb, which
is well worth seeing; while close by is a deep pit which
is generally partly filled with water. Near at hand too
is the modern Arab cemetery, which we have noticed
in another place. Farther to the south and over the
adjoining hill will be found a number of tombs which
are well worth a visit and are for the most part unknown to Mena residents.

During the last spring the authorities were opening
up a royal tomb at this spot—royal we were told it
was; and for days we went to look in the hope of
being allowed to see the finding of the sarcophagus.
We were always told it would not be yet. One day
a lady of our party discovered a large piece of painted
coffin which had been unearthed; in temper at its
being seen the attendant Arab smashed it to bits.
Still later we waited and returned one day to find
what we considered sure indications that the opening
was over; we should have done no harm, but anti-
quarian research is an impossible idea to the Arabs;
the only interest in this world according to their
view is that of paltry gain.

Returning homewards there are the relics of the large causeway along which if report be true were brought all the huge stones wherewith to build. We refrain from noticing other details of interest, except to point out the remains of the temple belonging to the smaller pyramid still standing to the south-east of that of Cheops. Not far too from this may be found a tomb in which is the carefully wrought cartouche of that mighty king.

A great deal of interest may be gained by a visit also to the tombs in the hill side immediately over-looking the adjacent village. We have endeavoured briefly to point out how much there is to see apart from and beside the better known show-places men-tioned fully in every guide book.

CHAPTER VII.

WHILE gazing upon the scene around the Pyramids, we have often wondered how things looked in the days of the ancient empire. The same brilliant light enwrapped all around, and made the same striking contrasts of sunshine and shade. The desert was there with its expanse of undulating trackless sand; the same green of luxuriant verdure in the Nile valley made a pleasing foreground to the lilac tinted hills behind. But surely there was something more attractive than this monotonous stretch of untidy and uneven ground, strewn with fragments of bones and of coffins, and interspersed with awkward-looking remnants of sepulchres, and gaping shapeless pits, and surface dips, which are exactly like pools of sand; something more worth looking at than these rough partly ruined Pyramids, surrounded by endless mounds of rubbish heaps; surely some other atmosphere pervading this great cemetery of kings, than the general air of neglect and desertion which now so pathetically envelops what remains. There must have been some brightness and neatness and order, some appearance of life and action, of trees and vegetation about this district which contained the royal mauso-

D 2

leums of the monarchs of one of the greatest of empires, instead of the present squalor and wretchedness, which the ever drifting sand only half covers up. It would be a relief to many minds if something could be done towards making things look respectable by clearing away the mountains of sand which have drifted where they were never meant to be; and if some attempt could be made to bring about a general excavation such as that which laid Pompeii bare.

We can imagine the scene as it existed of old— everywhere order and careful arrangement with no rubbish or refuse; even the sand kept from encroaching by dint of strenuous care; the Sphinx and Temple standing out in solemn majesty; the Pyramids aglow with gold and colour; the many other temples resplendent with paint and wondrous architecture and graceful statuary; tombs of all kinds, properly tended and cared for amid avenues of palm trees; constant processions of stately priests trained in all the dignified ritual of mysterious rites; everywhere life and activity; crowds of Egyptians visiting on a holiday, or on many other occasions the tombs of their kings and statesmen—just as nowadays people go to see the tombs at Westminster Abbey or St. Paul's —and, what is more, many a group of sorrow-stricken survivors arriving to pay the last mark of respect to departed relations or friends; men, such as Abraham and Joseph and Moses, coming to gaze upon one of the most impressive scenes that the world could produce. Are we wrong in our dream that pomp and splendour of all kinds once surrounded the Pyramids? We venture to think we are right.

We may grieve for the cruelty which could make so many lose their lives while working at the erection of tombs, which were to satisfy the pride and conceit of one or two men, but we may be sure that a people who thought so much about the state after death, and who called their homes only "hostels," but their graves "eternal habitations," must always have found a supreme attraction in the spot where were situate the grandest of tombs. If the population of ancient Egypt was somewhere about 6,000,000, as Lane seems to think, then we may be confident that the scene around the Pyramids was one of active interest.* That cemetery was one of the world's grandest conceptions. Even in all its present degradation the pathos of it leaves an ineradicable impression on the mind, and as we think upon all that has been, we can but say "Ichabod," for the glory has indeed departed.

---

* One remark we would make. A large cemetery presupposes the existence of a large *town*. Although we have little doubt that Egyptians were brought from many other parts of the kingdom to be buried near the resting place of mighty Cheops, still we have often thought that the large number of interments in the neighbourhood points to the fact that Memphis was a city of very considerable size, even larger than is commonly supposed.

CHAPTER VIII.

BIBLE INCIDENTS EXPLAINED.

THE natural home of conservatism is the East, where manners, ways, and customs are the same now as they were thousands of years ago. The rule of fashion is supreme, but the fashion is one and unchanging. From father to son traditions are handed down; it would be a crime to suggest that the children could know more than their parents, or that modern ways could surpass the older ones. Change, in one sense, there has been—by one nation after another Egypt has been conquered; Greeks and Romans, Persians and Arabs, French and English have gained the upper hand, and have made some impression on the conquered race—and yet all the winds of alteration, which have swept over the land, have after all, left the quiet unobtrusive country life virtually unaffected. Slow is the pace at which things alter, and the ancient Egyptians probably tilled their land, and reaped their harvests, in much the same way as do the Fellahin at the present day. Rulers have come and gone; dynasties have begun and ended; nation after nation has tried its hand at governing the country: but still much of the old life survives. Even faces are much the same, and many a donkey boy has features like the statue of

Rameses II., and many a memory of the monuments is awakened by the street scenes in Cairo to-day.

For those who are familiar with the language of the Bible, Eastern lands have a double charm. The life lived in them at the present time is in many ways an exact representation of scenes about which we have so often read. The Bible is an Eastern book ; the incidents and events it relates all bear an Eastern tinge ; the manners and customs of its heroes and heroines have a significance, when viewed in an Eastern light, which no amount of European knowledge can explain. The life described in the Scriptures was much more like that which may be witnessed in Egypt at the present day than the conventional presentations with which our English eyes are familiar. Egypt differs little from Palestine itself in habits and way of thought.

One fact which is ever being specially forced upon us is that in Egypt women occupy quite a subordinate position. It is the men who are all-important ; they are the richly dressed persons, and alone are thought worthy of consideration. The "rule of contrary" is worked out under many forms, and the exact opposite of English notions is the custom of the land. As a point of correctness the head is often shaved while the beard is generally allowed to grow ; shoes are removed out of reverence to holy ground or otherwise, while to take off the head covering is an act of disrespect ; writing is made to go from right to left ; in beckoning anyone to come to him, an Eastern motions from himself to the other party ; carriages in meeting take the right side, in passing

take the left : as a rule, if one of two must walk, it is
the man who rides, while the woman has to keep pace
by his side ; women are the drudges, and do the hard
work, and the men rest in idleness, conscious of their
handsome looks ; it is the reverse of good breeding to
enquire after a man's wife ; women uniformly veil
their faces, and specially the mouth, in the presence of
men ; but it is not considered immodest for them to
show the ancle, or even part of the leg.

Many other incidents which anyone may notice for
himself bear a still greater likeness to the ways of life
in Bible history.

The low oblong "black tents" of the Bedouin
tribes, dotted down upon the plain in some spot where
forage is abundant, are one and the same with the
"encampments" of old. These striped, rag-patched
homes of camels-hair canvas are probably much the
same as those in which the Patriarchs lived. After
residence for a period in one spot, the camels and flocks
and herds are collected together, the tents are struck, and
with all the furniture are placed on the camels' backs,
and the whole tribe moves on to fresh ground.
Arrived there, once more the tents are pitched, and
life goes on as usual for a time. It is a strange sight
to inspect the inside of these desert dwellings ; the
women's part is curtained off from that of the men ;
crowds of children surround the tents ; the head of
the tribe receives strangers with great grace, but is by
no means above receiving backsheesh. A Bedouin
Shékh, mounted on his camel, adorned with its many
rich trappings, his head and body swathed in an
ample white shawl, over which is flung the large

black cloak, with his long-barrelled rifle in his hand, and his general warlike look, has probably the the same appearance as had Abraham of old. Women come twice daily—this task is never performed by men—to draw water at the stone wells of the desert or the village, with their waterpots poised upon their heads. This habit of bearing weights upon the head conduces to the erectness of stature, for which Egyptian women are famed. It may not be generally known that to lift one of these pots, when filled, and to place it on the head, requires all the strength of a man.

The rock-hewn tombs cut in the hill sides, comfortable dwelling-places too, cool in summer and warm in winter, are very much like those in which people lived in our Lord's time. The tomb of Macpelah in which Abraham and Sarah were buried still remains in Hebron, and probably that place of sepulture was very much like many of the tombs with hollowed-out body-recesses, which may be seen any day round the Pyramids.

The houses are mostly flat-roofed, and on these "house-tops" people sit and enjoy the air. To such an extent are they used, that it has been remarked that blind men are generally chosen to mount the minarets of the mosques of an Eastern city, and give the call to prayer, that they may not overlook all that takes place on these roofs ; many of the poorer houses and hovels in the villages round Mena have no roofs at all, save the sugar-canes or "flax-stalks," which are laid on end, so as to keep out the sun, protection against rain being hardly needed. Pigeon cots will be found in every village—tower-like domes of mud, with palm-branches sticking forth from the walls—and round these "the doves" whirl and circle in all the joy of freedom. The same rough and primitive ploughs are used now as in the days of old ; to them sometimes may be seen animals "unequally yoked ; " a camel and a donkey do not look well in this connection, more especially as a camel is properly not a beast of draught, but of burden, and, therefore, for such purposes is seldom used.

Oxen still tread out the corn, with a kind of wooden roller, and, while doing this, the law as to their being unmuzzled seems to prevail.   Little children often may be seen leading a whole string of camels, the strange, unloving, yet submissive faces of the latter being a striking sight.   The shepherd of the flock still goes before the sheep, meek and mild-looking creatures with long pendent ears, who follow him wherever he leads.   Goat-skins, retaining the form of the animal's legs and body, with all the rough hair still attached, are used as water-bags, wherewith to water the roads.   Skins, akin to these, once formed the "bottles," which new wine would surely burst.   Saises or "fore-runners," clad in gor-geous running robes, go before the carriages of the great, carrying long wands, and crying out that the way must be cleared in front.   The outer cloaks which all the natives wear, are useful for many purposes ; men often lie down on them as a bed, or use them as carpets for prayers ; it was these cloaks which the Jewish pawnbrokers were bidden to restore at night. The beds on which the people sleep, are simply

ARAB WITH WATER-SKIN.

(By permission, from a photograph by Zangaki.)

mattresses often placed on a bedstead made of clay. They are quite light, and can easily be taken up, and carried. The houses are generally built of mud, and could certainly be easily swept away, if at any time the rain descended, and the floods came, and the winds blew, and beat upon them. There is, too, the sand, in which treasures could easily be buried, of which, indeed, we see evidence all around. There are the birds ever wheeling round, ready to pounce on the stray carcase, which may have, for a few minutes only, dotted the yellow sand. There are the valleys, which are full of bones—"bones which are very dry." Dogs of savage appearance prowl round the villages night and day—dogs which are nought but scavengers, scorned and despised, fierce and morose, ready, at any time, to eat a Jezebel up. Shoes are easily removed, when the sanctity of place demands ; so too can the loose outer cloaks be taken off, and together with palm-branches, strewn in the way over which great men are about to ride. It is quite dignified for high officials to ride on donkeys, and the sight may often be seen of mother and child on donkey-back, and the father walking by the side— like Joseph of old, accompanying the Virgin with the Holy Child. Women are often to be seen grinding at the mill. Children are trained, at least in outward show, to obey their parents in all things. The teacher sits on the ground in the midst of his scholars, just as the Lord "sat and taught" surrounded by His Apostles. In any village quarrel, dust is freely thrown in the air, and the rending of the clothes would not be an unknown sight. "Locusts and wild honey" could form a very

acceptable diet ; and one understands how, in the
desert, thieves could easily " dig " through, and steal
the possessions, which are generally in the form of
gold and silver bracelets, anklets, jewelry, and raiment.
One realises, too, the value of a " hiding-place
from the wind," and " a covert from the tempest," and
" the shadow of a great rock in a weary land." It is
significant to remember how the Israelites, who had,
we may feel sure, so often heard of and seen the
Pyramids, sick and weary of the desert life in Arabia
after their miraculous deliverance from Egypt, must
have thought the fertile Nile valley was better
to live in, albeit as slaves, and how in grumbling des-
pair they sighed after " the cucumbers and the melons,
the leeks and the onions," and asked Moses, if there
were " no *graves* in Egypt," that he must needs bring
them into that joyless barren waste to die.

CHAPTER IX

IT is well to remember that the Pyramids were not built by the Israelites, but had long previously existed ; and, to be chronologically correct, we must think of those monuments as upwards of a thousand years old when Abraham came upon the scene. We may be astonished when we think of the Pyramids as having been built some six or seven thousand years ago ; but it is a far more difficult question as to what would be the age of those fossilized remains of living creatures which form the very stone of the plateau on which the Pyramids themselves are built ; the span of man's existence on the globe, so far as known to history, occupies but a few years after all.

When the Pyramids were of a respectable antiquity, and Cheops had been resting in his coffin for a considerable time, some unsettling of the natives in Chaldæa was the secondary cause of bringing Abraham to Syria ; from thence he passed on to Egypt, and after remaining there for a time withdrew to Palestine, where he and Sarah were buried and where, it is believed, their bodies still remain.

The coming of Abraham was the first of the connecting links between the history of ancient Egypt and the Bible, and took place probably somewhere about the twelfth dynasty. Several kings' reigns were included in a dynasty, the duration of which may roughly be said to be rather over one hundred years; Cheops, who built the great Pyramid, lived in the fourth dynasty ; eight lines of kings had therefore come and gone since his time when Abraham came. He must have found on his arrival an advanced state of civilization, if not a civilization of which the climax had been already passed ; for here the curious nature of Egyptian history comes in, that the earlier the dynasty the higher seems to have been the pitch at which art and culture had arrived ; but how many centuries prepared the way for that refinement of civilization which certainly existed in the fourth dynasty, as may be witnessed in the Gizeh museum, we dare not say.

Almost alone the Father of the Faithful entered the land, but ere long in large numbers his descendants came to it. Years had gone by, and the chosen family had grown ; the eleven brothers hated the younger, and by their means Joseph was sold to a party of Midianite merchants travelling by the caravan route from Damascus to Egypt. Friendless he entered the land in which, by a providential chain of circumstances, he rose gradually to eminence. Steward and overseer of his master's house, favourite in the city prison, interpreter of dreams to the king, prime minister and sole administrator of the country, the ' saviour ' and protector of the people,—such were the honours to which he attained. He, of course, saw the Pyramids, for the numerous offices which he filled would of necessity bring him in personal touch with all places in the dominions as he travelled about to see what could be done to stem the tide of famine, which resulted from a continuance of low risings of the Nile. Had we been by the Pyramids in those days—we say it with all reverence—we might have driven over to Heliopolis close by Cairo (the On of Scripture) to see the wedding between Joseph the Premier and Asenath the daughter of Potipherah, one of the high-born priests of the Egyptian faith.

The pressure of the famine, which seems too to have been felt in other lands, brought the brethren of Joseph and his aged father into Egypt. We need not repeat the story of those wonderful chapters, of which every detail fits in with what has been discovered and is now known of Egyptian life. They were bidden to dwell in the land of Goshen, and to make their habitation somewhere not far from Ismailia.

The date at which Joseph rose to this high position was probably under the Hyksos or Shepherd dynasty. The kings of that line had wrested the crown from the old Egyptian blood royal, and among them was most likely that ruler, a shepherd himself, who showed such a willingness to promote Joseph, who was come of a race at once pastoral and akin to his own. This solution seems accepted by all the great writers on Egypt,* and it certainly explains the cause of a foreigner rising to such a supremely important position.

After another long spell of silence in the Bible record, during which years had gone by, Jacob's sons and

---

* Birch, Prugsch, Maspero, Wiedemann, and Sayce.

F

their families had become a nation, and all the favourable conditions were changed. The Pharaoh was actively hostile. The old days when Joseph's name was one to which honour and respect were due had gone for ever. Only a grinding slavery existed for those descendants, who as a pastoral race might be supposed to be in favour with the Shepherd kings, who had in their turn been driven out by the old Egyptian race. The growing numbers of the Israelites had become a positive danger, and hence the hard rule was enacted that all the male children should be destroyed. Slavery now began in earnest. Work was the order of the day. Everywhere the Israelites were scourged into carrying on ceaselessly those great building operations of which the ruins still remain. Under Seti I. and under Rameses his son the bitterness of bondage was felt : in the morning the people longed for night, and in the evening they longed for day ; hardly bearable was their daily round of toil. Then came the episode of the birth and finding of Moses. Events shaped their course to favour the prospects of the Hebrew boy ; reared in the royal palace, cared for by a royal princess, he grew learned in all the wisdom of the Egyptians, and doubtless went to the university of Heliopolis, then greatly renowned ; and so gained the training which fitted him for his future arduous task as Prophet, Ruler, and Lawgiver.

But his people were still brick-making slaves, ever at work for their hated lords. The building operations on which they were engaged were according to the Bible authority the erection of the treasure cities Pithom and Raamses. By recent laborious investigation the remains of these very cities have been discovered hidden far beneath the sand. The excavations brought to light the foundations of the town of Pi-Tum (Pithom), situate somewhere near Tel-el-Kebir. For the building of these cities bricks were used. These bricks, some of which are in the British Museum and are stamped with the name of Rameses II., may have been the very ones made by the Israelites of old.

Moses had by this time grown up, and seeing one day an instance of oppression displayed by an overseer towards one of his brethren, in his indignation rose up and slew the man, and hid his body in the sand. But he had done a dire act ; his life was in danger, and he had to flee. For years he stayed in Midian, in the south, not daring to return. At last Rameses died, and Moses came back, to be the liberator of his people. His first appeal was received with haughty contempt. In course of time the plagues followed, which were probably spread over several months—the darkness of the sandstorm which might be felt ; the unusual prevalence of frogs, and lice, and flies and locusts ; the breaking out of the skin disease; the downpour of hail ; the death of the first-born. Residence in Egypt suggests how dreadful these things might be.

In haste the Pharaoh had bidden them go forth from Goshen. They set out eastward, and marched to the bitter lakes, whose waters were probably then joined to the Red Sea below, somewhere near the modern Ismailia. In safety they crossed, while their oppressors perished in the waves. Some seem to

think that possibly king Menepthah stayed at home,
and so escaped death on that occasion. In the
Gizeh Museum at Cairo, under glass cases, exposed
to every vulgar stare, lie the remains of those old
kings whom Moses dared at his peril to withstand.
The mummied forms of Seti and of Rameses, in all
their ghastly glory, still repose in their last long sleep.
The bodies of these old monarchs, who were the
terror of their times, whose word was law, and who
were supposed to be half divine, have been ruthlessly
dragged forth from their secret resting places, treated
with but scanty respect, and are now looked on as
curiosities of a certain interest—*sic transit gloria
mundi !*

CHAPTER X.

THE BAZAARS IN CAIRO.

To ride on a donkey, or to be driven through the streets of Cairo is a delight.* The Mouski is the representative street; narrow even now, but broad compared with what it once was. Above is the sky of cloudless blue, while the street itself is in shade broken by occasional gleams of brightest sunshine. On either side smaller streets and still narrower passages open out.

The upper stories of the houses generally project, while the windows of moushrabeah work reach still farther forward, until in many of the narrow lanes the houses nearly seem to touch. The dark wood of these windows placed against the light-coloured walls; the pink and white striped mosques, which everywhere abound; the artistic appearance presented by the architecture in general, and in particular by the finely tapering minarets; and the Eastern tone which

---

* The usual way of sight-seeing, and visiting the bazaars in Cairo is on donkeys. The authorized Police tariff for these, and for hackney carriages, can be obtained at the Zaptieh, or Police Bureau. Visitors would save themselves the trouble and annoyance of over-charges, by obtaining a copy of the tariff on their arrival in Cairo. The regulation price for a carriage is from six to eight piastres an hour, equal, in English money, to about 1/6.

seems to pervade all things—all go to make the scene in Cairo one never to be forgotten.

On the roadway of the Mouski itself is a never-ending panorama of moving human forms. Types of every kind of inhabitants may be found there; all chattering, bargaining, complaining, or singing to themselves. Merchants sleek and fat, clad in wondrous combinations of subdued colours; stately Bedouins in black and white; Fellahs in blue with bare feet and brown caps; Nubians with black, shiny faces well set on their shapely bodies, handsome well-made men, tall and dignified; negroes with a wealth of grinning teeth; women with a down-trodden look shuffling along in their dress of dark blue; grander ladies in veil of white and encased in the balloon-like cloak, walking or on donkeys, but all looking awkward and fat, some even driving in English broughams of the most modern type; dragomans in wondrous baggy trousers; boys with sad, intelligent faces leading noble-looking donkeys harnessed with bright-red saddles and bedecked with tinkling brass chains.

In the general medley, cooped up in the narrow way also, are dogs appearing to have tempers which never could be made sweet, and to possess a close relationship to wolves; camels laden with huge loads, now of sugar canes, now of planks or stones, caring little for the dire confusion their passage causes; poor, weak-looking donkeys loaded with more than they can bear; water-carriers with artistic, brass-bound jars; lemonade-sellers giving notice of their approach by the clinking of the brass cups they carry; sellers of sweetmeats, sellers of oranges,

IN THE BAZAARS, CAIRO,

(By permission, from a Photograph by Zangaki.)

sellers of cigarettes, all howling out their business in
a melancholy street cry ; podgy officials in scarlet
fez and European black coat ; still grander Pashas
driving in carriages with gaily dressed servants on
the box ; tourists and visitors of every nationality ;
beggars, mostly blind, and always dirty, screaming
for a stray piastre ; people of every hue and dressed
in every fashion.   Such is the scene the Mouski
presents.

Arrived at the Bazaars, we find still further
wonders. Those who have been to Damascus tell
us that the bazaars of Cairo present a genuine
Eastern appearance which is nowhere surpassed.
Each trade has its own special bazaar, and is
probably represented by many shops. In that
bazaar nothing else can be bought. The shops
themselves are open to the street, and are about the
size of and somewhat like the window of one
of our very small shops with the glass removed.
On the raised floor of these shops the merchants sit
surrounded by their goods, which present to the
eye in many cases a charming assortment of colour.
The lanes of the bazaars are very narrow, and are
crowded with passers-by, sometimes diseased and
dirty, who jostle you at every turn.

As one passes along, quite a bewildering scene of
variety presents itself : so many are the things
exposed to view for sale. Crockery of all shapes,
design, and colour ; saddlery, gleaming with a general
tone of red ; bespangled embroidery beautifully
made and worked with gold or silver ; fezzes of
spotless scarlet carefully blocked and trimmed ;

slippers in yellow, and slippers in mauve or red, with
pointed turned-up toes ; firearms and weapons of
many kinds, some of wondrous inlaid work and
antique design, some quite new and ready for
butchery to come ; swords with inscribed blades ;
daggers in leather sheaths ; pipes red and white,
and brown ; spices, and seeds, and powders of every
colour and shade ; sweetmeats pink, and sugary, and
horrible to behold ; examples of the many uses to
which the moushrabeah wood-work can be put ;
odds and ends of all kinds ; children's dresses and
gay-coloured handkerchiefs, startling in design and
mostly manfactured in Manchester ; toys and fabrics
of every sort and description and make.

Some of the shops are redolent with the odour of
wonderful scents, above which tiny streamers of gold
and silver foil flutter in the wind and make a soft
musical sound. Some display goods of gold and
silver workmanship and trays of priceless gems ; while
others are rich in beautifully inscribed brass work and
a wealth of carpets and rugs.

Should the owner desire to go to mosque to say his
prayers, he leaves everything just as it is, only hanging
a net in front of all to signify he is away. If he be
there and ready to sell, a purchase is not a very
speedy matter, though we have been told he will
think twice before refusing the first offer of the
day. Our first request to know the price of any
particular article is met by a counter request to sit
down in the shop ; after a time coffee and cigarettes
arrive, and a conversation goes one ; we signal to our
dragoman that we want to get to business ; the

merchant persists in showing us many other things first. At last we determine to know the price of what we want ; of course, it is exorbitant, and we offer very much less ; the shopman evinces amusement and contempt, and we depart. Before we have gone far, however, we are summoned back, and the bargaining is repeated ; his price comes down, and our offer rises ; possibly, someone else will enter the fray, and take the merchant's part, and all the while beggars persistently bother us. At last we warn our dragoman he must bring things to a close, and that we shall give no more than we have offered. The bargain is at last concluded, and we feel confident that we have been swindled after all ; if we are wise, we demand backsheesh before departing : a concession which the merchant, knowing that he has made a good profit, can well afford to give ; we retreat at last, half wondering whether the purchase has been worth the trouble.

After constant practice we found that we became so inured to the ordeal that we grew quite bold in our demands, and obtained what we desired after a period of haggling which, considering we were in the East, was brief indeed.

CHAPTER XI.

MORE CAIRO SIGHTS.

THERE are several Coptic churches which are well worth a visit. The way to them is a dusty one, leading to old Cairo, where they may be found mostly situate in the ' Ders ' or walled-in districts which are inhabited by the Copts. A wealth of paintings of saints, remarkably well done, grace the walls of these churches, while inlaid work abounds in pulpit or in screen ; in arrangement and in ' oldworldism ' they are very interesting.

Whether the story that the Holy Family came to the region of the pyramids, in their flight from Herod's wrath be true or not, is not a matter for us here to enter on.

To Egypt the Infant Christ was taken ; and it is almost certain that His parents would in that land have made for the abode of Jews ; a determination which may very likely have brought them into the region of Cairo.

The tradition tells that Mary and Joseph and the Divine Babe, on entering Egypt, came to Heliopolis, where a tree is still shown, marking the spot where, in the well hard by, the Virgin washed the travel-stained clothes ; from Heliopolis they passed to Cairo, and there for a time remained.

Around one of the oldest of the Coptic churches in Cairo, that of Aboo Sergah, hangs the odour of sanctity, for in an ancient stone vault, below the floor of the present church and far below the level of the modern city, is shown the resting-place of the Holy Child and His Mother.

Certainly the Citadel must be seen. Arrived at the summit of the crag on which it stands, you find a perfect view of the city and the river and the Mokattam hills behind. It was from the Citadel rock that the Memlook took his memorable leap, and landed at the bottom unhurt. The mosque of Mehemet Ali, built, let us hope, in expiation of evil deeds, is beautiful in its way with its alabaster walls and lovely carpets and a wealth of lamps which hang like gold fish globes from the roof. It is new, and therefore in better order than other mosques, and about the size of, and in someways not unlike, the Dome of St. Paul's.

We remember one night driving in from Mena to see the ceremony of the Leilit el Kadr, when the Khedive goes to this mosque to pray. By faulty information as to the time of service we arrived a little late, and met the Khedivial cavalcade returning to the Palace. We pressed on, however, and arrived in time to have the doors shut in our faces. Not even one fair look were we allowed to have, despite all our entreaties. We had driven ten miles out, and we had before us a drive of ten miles back. It was certainly a hardly bought experience, for from the glimpse we had of the interior we gathered that the effect of the building when lit up, about which so very much is said, was most ordinary after all.

The mosque of Sultan Hassan at the foot of the hill is one of the oldest of the lot, ragged, and in bad repair—for the Arabs erect new buildings, but never restore the old—but yet venerable in its wealth of malachite and marble. Some of the other mosques of the city are covered in and dark, while some are completely open to the air. The noted mosque of El-Azhar forms the University of Cairo, and is regarded as one of the most important of the Muslim schools. In the huge courtyard with its wealth of columns may be seen many a small circle of Arab boys clothed in a variety of colours, seated on the ground, and listening to their teacher, or committing portions of the Koran to memory. That of El Touloun is a huge quadrangle open to the sky and surrounded by a cloister which alone is roofed. Reiterated visits to them grow monotonous, for there is a sameness about them all and an emptiness which we do not admire: though the *kibla* or niche-like 'east end' and the pulpit are often superbly decorated with marble, and the walls are lined with coloured tiles.

Before all things else in interest comes the wonderful Gizeh Museum. The gardens in which it stands are well worth a visit, laid out with true Eastern magnificence. But the marvels of the interior are unsurpassed. We have alluded elsewhere to the most important mummies ; once we remember going into a small room where many of these swathed forms, not yet ticketed and labelled, were lying around ; by the scent of the room it was all too plain that even mummies will not keep for ever.

To the two well known statues of Ra-hetep and

Nefert we draw attention to remark upon their age and perfect execution. Dating probably from the time before the Pyramids were built, they yet display great finish. Very life-like is their expression, and it is due to the arrangement of the eyes, which are inserted in an eyelid of bronze ; the eyeball is of quartz, the iris of crystal, and the pupil looks like a nail-head in the centre ; but so perfect is the imitation that we felt in some way the figures must be instinct with life. Other statues there are of almost equal interest ; we refrain from mentioning more, except to advise a search for the dark diorite stone figure of Cephren, who built the second Pyramid, which was found in the Temple of the Sphinx, and the wooden statue of the Shêkh el beled, which looks life-like in its portly stateliness.

The jewelry in the museum is of perfect workmanship and beauty. There is plenty of it to be seen ; and the find that caused such a sensation in the spring of 1894 is said to be equal to, if not to surpass in excellence of finish, those productions for which Bond Street jewellers are nowadays greatly famed.

Hours may be passed in this most deeply interesting place, and still half of the wonders left unseen.

CHAPTER XII.

DRESS OF THE MODERN EGYPTIANS.

ROUGHLY we may divide the Mohammedan inhabitants into members of the higher class, and Bedouin and Fellahin. The complexion of the higher class of Egyptians is very much the same as that of a European ; while the coffee-coloured face of the Bedouin is thinner and less round than that of the Fellah, but it is often hard to distinguish them apart. The Coptic Christians, of which there are many, and who generally hold positions in the Government service, are supposed to represent the old Egyptian stock, and certainly their profile is at times not unlike the portraits delineated on the monuments—but intermarriage among the various sections of the population greatly obliterates the distinguishing features of all. The general dress of the Egyptian official is very much of a European cut ; he (and among the Copts this is specially noticeable) wears ordinarily a kind of black frock-coat of a clerical cut, his head being covered by an ordinary red fez.

Next to these officials, high or low, as the case may be, comes the class of the town merchants—gaily clad gentlemen they certainly are, often of large build, but with a fat, pasty-looking face. The dress worn by

them is purely Eastern, and is varied in colour, any
shade and combination they choose being permissible.
These merchants are generally clad in a dressing-
gown like garment reaching to the feet of striped silk
and bound round the waist with a handsome girdle—
over this robe, which has long sleeves, is worn a kind of
ordinary cloth coat, also reaching to the feet, generally
of one plain colour, subdued brown or blue, or mulberry
or maize ; the head is often shaved, and swathed in
a large turban of white or possibly green or yellow
muslin.   Such   is   the   dress   of   the   townsman   of
position.

The Bedouin is of a quite different race.   In his
own estimation he is a lordly gentleman, and it is
against his principle to dwell much in towns.   He is
supposed to belong to a race which lives in tents, and
to be a free-born son of the desert, whom none can
tame ; but circumstances are now greatly changed.
The one thing against which he revolts is military
conscription.   As a rule, his dress is a study in black
and white ; the plain calico cassock which he wears
displays a piece of the yellow waistcoat beneath ; but
he is fond of wrapping both head and body in the
ample folds of a voluminous finely spun Algerian
shawl.   Over this he will wear the black cloak, very
much like the gown of a college don, and will at
times tie a gaudy silk scarf on his head, with the ends
falling down over his shoulders and neck, and so
make himself look not altogether unlike the Sphinx.

The ordinary Fellah is the agriculturist, living in
the villages around.   He is a poorly clad person, his
clothes being often much torn and in rags.   His dress

F

is a kind of long blue shirt, under which appears at times a yellow or red waistcoat; if he has a girdle, it is of leather (like John the Baptist of old), and his head is covered with a brown felt skull cap, round which a white turban is sometimes bound. On some occasions he will wear a cloak of striped camels' hair, white and brown, of striking appearance. His whole dress is rough, and often dirty; his feet are unshod, and his person is not kept very clean. The dress of women of the lower class is always a kind of dark blue robe which hangs very loosely from the shoulders, and has very long sleeves; the head is covered with a black muslin handkerchief which hangs down far behind, and this they use to cover the mouth when need arises, for they often wear no other veil; their necks and ears are loaded with cheap but glittering ornaments.

The dress of the women of all classes is very much more sober than that of their lords. In the towns they wear over all else a dark blue and white sheet-like garment which wraps in head and dress as well, and makes them look like walking sacks; the eyes alone are visible, for all the rest of the face is thickly veiled in black. The grander ladies are generally more carefully dressed, sometimes in pink or other colour, with a white face-veil, but over head and dress alike is placed the usual large overall, in this case of black silk which fills out when the wind catches it, and makes their figures look like an inflated balloon. The ladies who are at the top of the social scale wear much the same, with the exception that the face-veil is of the thinnest muslin, and is scarcely a blind at all. The beauty of

VEILED ARAB WOMEN WITH WATERPOTS.

(By permission, from a photograph by Zangaki.)

F 2

the eyes of Egyptian ladies, all deeply painted round with "kohl," quite makes up for the hiding of their other features which are hidden by the veil.

Two more classes of men we must mention, and first the dragomans. They are of many nationalities, but the general arrangement of their dress is as follows : large baggy Turkish trousers, looking like a " divided skirt," drawn in at the ancles and very often of a brilliant hue ; a waistcoat of different and equally dazzling shade, and over that a short jacket very much like that of an Eton boy, of another gay colour ; over the head is arranged the handkerchief of silk—a gaudy dress it sounds to English ears, but then Easterns have an inborn facility for choice of colours which though brilliant, blend in exquisite accord, and never clash. One more class we must notice—the saises who run in front of carriages of great officials, and wear a striking garb. They are clothed in a thick, white, amply pleated muslin shirt and knicker-bockers, bound round the waist with a wondrous sash of gay coloured silk ; the braided sleeveless waistcoat generally of scarlet and gold, and the red skull cap, with an extra long tassel of blue, complete the get-up. The effect of these runners, as with their white sleeves and trousers, both made very full, showing off against their dark skin and legs bared below the knee, they run through the streets, clearing the way with their long wooden wands, is imposing in the extreme.

CHAPTER XIII.

HABITS AND CUSTOMS.

THE manners of the Arabs are certainly taking; graceful and courteous they naturally are and they walk with a studied bearing; they are mostly fine fellows and very fond of a joke, though their faces sometimes bear a sad and pathetic look; old age draws on very early, and then their ugliness is marked. Men's faces are often lined with scars, two or three parallel cuts having been made on the cheek, either for luck or so that their mothers might not mistake them; while their arms (and specially the chins and foreheads of the women) are often tattooed.

Where an Arab has the advantage, is in his beautiful dreamy eyes, and his perfect teeth; the latter, especially when first noticed, are striking by their cleanliness and spotless whiteness; the exact arrangement and absence of all decay, made us feel that artificial teeth in Egypt can seldom be in request.

We have been told that bone picking and meat tearing with the teeth is what we need to practice if the growing degeneracy of English teeth now-a-days is to be stayed. It may be the perpetual chewing and biting of sugar cane among the Arabs that conduces to the preservation of their teeth, certainly it seems to conduce to their strength. We tried with our feeble

masticators to tear some sugar cane one day ; we made
not the slightest impression but gave ourselves considerable pain ; and we found difficulty in cutting the
cane even with a knife, though they rend it like
orange peel.

The Bedouins make most excellent guides ; they
can, too, be very useful in helping you to climb ; and
the way in which by holding your arm on either side
they lift you easily over obstacles is charming to
experience. They are ever on the look out to sell you
some old bit of rubbish, or even modern imitations of
ancient curios, all the time declaring that they are
providing you with a genuine " anteeker " and that you
may indeed trust them. Their demeanour is usually
very calm, sedate and self composed, but they are
very much disinclined for work, except it be for
handsome pay. Their delight is to sit in the sun and
smoke. They wear shoes, it is true, but if any speed
be required in walking, they take them off and carry
them, thus shewing what their true idea of comfort is.
An Arab if he is well paid for it, will start from the
hotel, tear up the Pyramid, come down again, and
return to the hotel, all in about 12 minutes.*

A strict Mohammedan has an honest dread of being
photographed, for to make a picture of anything, is
forbidden by the Koran ; the aversion to it is of
course of necessity now gradually dying out, but he
who submits to have his picture taken, expects large
backsheesh in return.

---

* We believe the practice to be a very dangerous one, for such
sudden and violent exertion must cause a great danger of a chill if
nothing worse.

The conception of play and recreation hardly enters into the life of the Fellahin ; theirs is an existence of work for gain, and when that is attained of idleness ; amusement seems to be an idea not realisable, for the heart has been taken out of them by years of oppression. Things are better now, but the cringing down-trodden look remains. However hard they worked in the old bad days, they were always heavily mulcted in money or in kind, and had to give up much to their betters. The rapacious Pashas wanted money somehow, and so the Governors of the Provinces oppressed the Nazirs or mayors of the towns ; the Nazirs oppressed the Shékhs ; and the Shékhs ground down the Fellahin. We growl about a middleman in England ; in Egypt there were half a dozen middlemen, but the taxes are collected fairly and equitably now.

Dirt is not a thing which perturbs the poorer class very much. Their religion teaches them to wash, but the washing is often done in water which is used by all, and is never changed ; for the tanks in the courtyard of the mosque are replenished, but never cleaned out. The better class of persons are of course much more cleanly in their habits.

We have often asked the boys, why they wore such dirty clothes, when water was so cheap? the answer seemed to be, that washing wore the garment out. The girls are even worse than the boys, which may be attributed to the fact that they are engaged constantly in collecting manure wherewith to make fuel for the oven fires. The women too, have a very dirty look ; and the ugly fashion of staining the nails a brownish red colour with henna, is with them the height of fashion.

Mothers, we have been told, regard the washing of their infants until they are two years old as harmful to a degree; two years' dirt on a child is not a pleasant thought, and goes some way to account for the large infant mortality. They generally carry their children by placing them astride on their shoulders, and they quickly hide them if you look at them, fearing the evil eye. The same occult and baneful influence is feared for the camels, many of whom wear as a talisman, a portion of the Koran, which the owners feel must save them from harm. It is unlucky to drive away flies from the children's faces: we have often seen the eyes literally surrounded with them, and no effort taken to prevent it; it is therefore not to be wondered at that ophthalmia largely prevails.

Many of the Arabs are blind in at least one eye, and their blindness is very disfiguring, and makes them assume a piteous look. Cripples of all kinds too are to be seen, and they make their lameness an excuse for extorting backsheesh.

It is the custom of the villagers, if they have the chance, to ask Europeans to dinner, or at least to coffee, and presents are expected in return. We have never ourselves accepted these invitations, for we feared that the coffee might be boiled with water drawn from the village pond. We remember how once, when we were visiting a Bedouin encampment for a brief space, we gave as presents things that would please a child; the great shékh of the tribe

being delighted with a small hand mirror, in which he
viewed himself with glee.

One specially noticeable piece of furniture in Egypt
is the open wicker work frame, made in the shape of
a box, which does duty for so many things. These
frames are strongly and simply made, and adapted to
many purposes. They are used as bedsteads and
covered with a mattress, as divans, as seats, as book-
rests, as baskets, as cages, as tables, as provender bins,
as travelling boxes, and in other ways.

It is interesting to see a man climb the branchless
trunk of a date palm ; he places round the tree a loose
loop of rope, which is attached to his waist, and by
jerks he manages to raise himself, planting his feet
firmly against the stem until very quickly he is at the
top of the tree.

Bedouin and Fellahin alike are cruel. Far too
many sad sights have we seen to hesitate to say this,
Donkeys, staggering under a load of clover too heavy
for them to carry, are mercilessly beaten if they
stumble ; while often under the saddles which look so
nice their backs are painfully sore. For birds, and
beasts, and reptiles, and insects the natives seem not
to have any kind thoughts, unless it be for their own
camel or horse. Once we rescued a lynx, of course
by paying for its release, which was tightly bound
round the legs ; as we gave the money we threatened
our displeasure if the Arab tried this manœuvre to
get money again.

In many respects the ordinary inhabitants are
strangely patient and respectful of the law. We
remember from the top of the Barracks witnessing the

BRIDGE OVER NILE. CAIRO.

(By permission, from a photograph by Zangaki.)

state entry of his Highness the present Khedive, into Abdin Square, after his sudden accession to the throne. The official procession was followed by a surging mob which broke the line and threw all things into disorder. The police had hard work to keep back the crowd ; but the way in which they went to work was to hit as many as they could sharply on the head with a stick. In England those policemen would have met with opposition, but the Arabs took it very quietly.

On another occasion, near the Nile bridge, an old man got in the way of our victoria ; it is difficult indeed to make them move on one side ; and before we could prevent it, our driver had furiously lashed him over the shoulders with his whip. The severity of the blow made us shudder—the old man started and stared, but that was all.

We made it our business to study, as far as we could, the characters of the Arabs we came across, and for many of them we formed a great liking. Our guides Mohammed and Abdul Salam Dobree were all that we could wish.

Arabs have their faults, and they are many ; but we certainly found that with them as with all people in the world, kindness pays. We have sometimes heard apparent gentlemen speak to Arabs as if they were dogs ; that they can be annoying at times, we well know ; but after all they are human beings, with the same strange ambitions and sensibilities as our- selves ; and one who fails to recognise this will never understand the Arab nature. The Bedouin in a way considers himself a gentleman, and as such he ex-

pects to be humanely treated. If you want to get
real help from him—by treating him civilly alone will
you succeed. There must always be remembered the
difference of religion and race and ancestry. He sees
no wrong in what to you is mean and despicable;
and if you would convert him to your way of
looking at things, you must not despise the level to
which he has already attained. We say and we
believe it to be true, that when you have once won
an Arab's heart, you have gained in him an unwaver-
ing friend, who will serve you faithfully and well.

We have often seen the boys of Kafra enjoy a
game of football on the sands in the evening hour.
They play with unshod feet, and this says much for
the strength of their joints.

One day to Kafra there came a primitive merry-
go-round. It consisted of some rough wooden seats
which were swung round like a millwheel. The
preparing of proper sockets or the use of oil or grease
did not occur to the Arab mind, and the piteous
aggressive groaning of this awkward machine, while
hour after hour it was patronized by the boys we
shall never forget.

We wonder how the first few lines of the "Elegy
written in a Country Churchyard," would have been
adapted, had Gray had Egypt in his eye. Nearing
the hour of sunset, all the villagers may be seen
returning from their work; men and boys in brown
and white, going before flocks of peaceful looking
sheep and goats—women with baskets of tomatoes
on their heads—children riding ugly looking buffaloes
—grandly dressed men sitting astride small donkeys

—camels carrying loads of clover—all join in one long procession to the village gate.

We were much amused by a donkey boy, who had achieved the high honour of being sent on show to the World's Fair at Chicago. He had returned with the superior bearing acquired by travel, and with the dignified surname of Toby. His reply to our morning salutation was always "I'm all right, t'ank you. How's y'self?" We asked him whether he would have liked to remain in America. "No," he instantly replied, "I no wish to talk by my nose." The New World had clearly failed to impress the Old.

Arabs never can tell you how old they are; even the boys have no clear statement to convey to you as to their age or even their birthday. We remember asking one respectable-looking Arab, how many summers he had seen. He seemed in serious doubt, and solemnly replied he was not sure whether he was 49 or 94!

CHAPTER XIV.

CHRISTIAN AND MOHAMMEDAN OBSERVANCES.

EGYPT was once a Christian land. Its close proximity to Jerusalem made it one of the first countries to which the early preachers of the new faith came to convert people to the worship of a Greater than Osiris. Bishops, priests, and deacons abounded ; and those who know Kingsley's "Hypatia" will remember how important a Christian colony Alexandria became in later years.

The country submitted* to the Mohammedan conquest some years after the flight of Mohammed. The ancient Church, however, never died out, but continued to exist, and the ancient Egyptians are represented now by the Copts, though intermarriage of all kinds has prevented the distinctions of race from being very strictly kept. Persecution, bitter and severe, has swept over these Egyptian Christians ever since Diocletian's time. But to-day they still exist as a genuine body, and entitled in many ways to great respect. On their arms is generally tattooed the mark of the Cross. Proud of their ancestry, and clinging through all troubles to the faith, they were the first to welcome the protectorate of the English. Their liturgy is dignified and ancient, reaching back to the times of St. Mark ; and their ritual is very striking.

---

* About 640 A.D.

Their churches may be seen at many places in the country, in the midst of the ' Ders,' or fortified townships in which they still generally live.

It is true that their churches are dirty, their services somewhat irreverently performed, and their whole religion rather lifeless, but still in name and in practice they are Christians. The foundation has been laid, and though at the present time it seems that little can be done to raise them and give their priests a semblance of education, still in them is the nucleus of better things, and if Egypt is ever to become more largely Christian, most assuredly the power of the Coptic Church must not be ignored.

It was our privilege on the eve of the Epiphany Feast to attend one of their solemn gatherings at the new cathedral in Cairo. We started for the service about 9 p.m., and passing through the narrow streets and more or less crooked short cuts, we found the church fairly well filled.

On this one night in the year there was formerly observed a great ceremony of the blessing of the Epiphany tank of water, in which members of the congregation were plunged, in memory of the Baptism of the Lord. This rite has for various reasons ceased, and the only survival now is the special blessing of the people by the Patriarch, who signs them with the cross.

Like other Eastern churches the sanctuary is divided from the nave by a lofty screen which hides nearly all behind it from view. The building was lighted with candles, and there were two rows of choir boys, or acolytes, clad in white with gaily decorated scarves. All were bare-footed, as in the presence of God, and wore the red fez.

The Patriarch—an old man of no very prepossessing appearance—was there, clad in a gorgeous cope of blue and gold. To this was attached a tasselled hood which he wore during the service. The old man swayed in his walk, and the constant swinging to and fro of the tassel from his hooded head resembled the motion of a pendulum. Attendant bishops were there standing round the altar in equally gorgeous robes and surrounded by assistant priests, some of them with heads covered right through the service.

The singing of the choir was not inspiring. An elderly man kept the others in order and accompanied the music with the clash of cymbals, no organ being allowed in Eastern worship. In the middle stood the desk on which was placed the Gospels.

From behind the screen from time to time the Patriarch appeared to give the benediction with his cross. The Kyrie was solemnly sung, and the Gospel read first in Coptic by an official in ordinary dress, and after that in Arabic by a deacon who chanted it clearly to the people. The mass with its attendant ceremonies was duly celebrated. We were only able to stay for part of the service. After we left we were told there was a long sermon preached. The whole function gave us much to think about, and despite the seeming perfunctoriness which somewhat marred the effect, we felt we had witnessed worship which in many points was like that of the Apostolic days.

After this service, which was so clearly Christian, it was strange to go out into the streets and feel that

MOHAMMEDANS AT PRAYER.

(By permission, from a photograph by Zangaki.)

after all we were in a thoroughly Mohammedan land ; for although in Egypt there are many Coptic Christians, the prevailing religion of the country is that of Mohammed. Christianity once held sway with a vigorous Church, but the dissensions of parties, among other causes, made way for the Arab conquest. The outward expression of Mohammedanism is attractive ; drunkenness is looked upon as horrible, and a special Christian failing ; forms of prayer are rigidly practised in public rather than private ; though the instances of Arabs spreading their cloak by the way side and praying are less frequent than they were.

The mosques are often crowded, especially on Fridays, by whole rows of worshippers apparently absorbed, who prostrate themselves on the mats. Mohammedans constantly read the Koran, and tell their rosaries, and keep the stated fasts and feasts. They have a respect for most of the Jewish and even many of the Christian saints, and agree with Christians in many ways, but they hold a faith of a distinctly lower order, and there are dark spots in their practice ; their often brutal treatment of women, and the facility for divorce ; the hard, chilling fatalism ; the utter want of spirituality ; the lack of appreciation of truthfulness ; the degraded tone of morals ; the failure to make religion sanctify the life—these, and many other things made us feel only too well where they come short. Their reverence for Allah is supreme : and there is ever present to their minds the dread of incorrect thought about His unity. They constantly repeat, as if in terror of forgetting it, " there is no God but One."

Missionaries, we are told, work among Mohammedans generally with wonderfully small success. Into the reasons for this failure we dare not venture to intrude, but one thing we say :—If the conversion of Muslims to the Christian faith is to be achieved, it will only be by the missionary primarily stating the fact that while Muslim and Christian worship the same God, " Allah, the merciful, the compassionate," yet the Christian can teach the Muslim a better way to pray, through the merits of Him who was alike God and man.

The exaggerated fervour of worship, which is practised among some of the derwishes, is an excrescence on the ordinary state of religion, and corresponds to the vagaries of the " Salvation army" among ourselves. We went one night to see a thanksgiving service on an important occasion, close by Mena. Lamps swung from the roof of the tent which had been specially erected. When we arrived we found in the dim light about sixty men of whom some were derwishes. Forming themselves into two long rows they faced each other, and began their strange devotions. Two musicians playing on a kind of flute produced most mournful music, very much like that of bagpipes in distress. The monotonous wail seemed to excite those who were present to a pitch of fervour. They jumped as if they were hung on wires, and all the time hardly lifted their feet from the earth. With perfect drill they rolled their heads from side to side, and then swayed their bodies forwards and backwards. They knelt and did the same. They rose up and faced the music, and then turned sharply round. This continued right through the evening, everyone meanwhile uttering a deep guttural staccato 'Allah.' At times one of the number would get worked up to a pitch of frenzy ; then totter the whole length of the tent, and, with eyes glaring and nostrils dilated, violently roll against the rest, who somehow saved him from falling. Until he recovered he was laid flat on the ground. The whole thing was a continual repetition. We admired their simple faith which expressed itself in the utterance of the " High and Holy Name"; but how a great Englishman once brought himself to speak with favour of this kind of worship we certainly cannot tell.

It was by courtesy, we were told, that we were allowed to be present—we who were but "dogs of Christians" amidst the true believers :—it was a fact with which we had yet hardly learned to deal, that a Muslim looks with contempt upon the members of every other faith.

A funeral in Egypt is a quaint, mournful spectacle, taking place sometimes on the same day as the death. About six blind or decrepit men lead the procession, chanting their melancholy requiem. Then follow the male friends and relatives of the deceased ; possibly among them being some derwishes who carry green flags on poles. Then comes the open bier in which the body is laid covered with a large cloth or pall, the head being carried foremost. Behind this come the women in abject grief, making an awful wailing. The body itself is simply laid in the sand, and the mourners return. At the funeral of a great man the display is grander :

the procession being **headed by** camels laden **with bread and** water for distribution to the poor.

The Ramadan Fast **is very** strictly **kept.** We once asked a Bedouin **what would be the** penalty if **a Muslim refused to obey the fasting** rule. 'If a man **no keep** Ramadan, **he go** hell,' **was the** man's simple **reply. His** religion was **at least a** practical one. Certainly **there is a universal** agreement that **the fast has an irritating effect upon the** temper. **The** heavy meals **taken during the night in part** make **up for the strain endured in the day; but also** bring about **the result that the men are lazy and indisposed for** work, **for from sunrise to sunset Muslims neither eat,** nor **smoke, nor drink. We recall how on one of the days of the Ramadan month we had taken an Arab** with **us to Sakkarah ; the morning was intensely hot, and our guide ran the greater part of the way, a good ten miles ; even we who had driven were parched by noon ; but until the gun from off the Citadel at sunset had flashed forth the intelligence that** the fast **was done, not one drop of liquid would he let pass his lips. We could but admire such strong consistency and obedience to his faith.**

When once Ramadan is over, the Feast of Bairam begins. The Arabs explained its festival nature to us by calling the first day of it their 'Christmas.' Certainly they make much of it, donning new clothes and putting on holiday attire. We were told that on that morning the telegraph offices are crowded by Arabs who send messages of congratulation to their friends. Telegraphic good wishes will perhaps with us one day supersede Christmas cards.

In the early hours of Bairam morning an interesting ceremony takes place. The people keep the occasion as a kind of All Souls' Day, and in a body go to visit the graves of departed friends. We joined the company at the cemetery close by Kafra. The scene looked like a village fair: sweet-stalls abounded, and boys were shooting with toy guns, or blowing india-rubber squeakers. The elder people had taken to the graves palm boughs and flat cakes of bread—these latter being provided by the well-to-do for their poorer brethren. Prayers were said at the tombs, and good wishes exchanged. Men and women alike seemed in high good humour. By eight o'clock on that lovely April morning the opening ceremony of Bairam was over.

CHAPTER XV.

COUNTRY SCENES.

In Egypt, we may fairly say, no rain ever falls; the showers when they come are very brief, and spread as they are over the few winter months, could probably be compressed into 24 hours' rainfall.

The one source of fertility is the Nile. In July the rise begins, and as the overflow is good or bad so will next year's harvest be a success or failure. The need for Egypt is by some feat of engineering to collect the water when the river is in flood and there is such an abundant supply, and to prevent it being so rapidly carried away to the sea. Schemes for that purpose are under consideration at the present moment.

Some of the water left from the overflow is now retained by means of ponds and canals of which there are many in the valley. From these the water is raised by "sakiehs" or "shadoofs," and poured into the channels whence by a wonderful arrangement of connecting furrows it is dispersed broadcast over the fields. Very pretty it is to watch the water that has perhaps come from some distance, coursing along in its narrow groove, and meanwhile nourishing every inch of the cultivated land over which it pours.

The sakieh is the larger arrangement of the two.

It consists of a wheel which is turned by a donkey or a buffalo ; to this wheel pots are attached, which continuously raise the water, the whole machine all the while making a queer melancholy groaning sound which is audible from some distance off.

The shadoof is a simpler arrangement, and is worked by men. A post is fixed in the bank of the pond or canal, and on this is poised a thick cumbersome kind of pole, which will move up and down. To one end of this pole a heavy stone is attached ; to the other a piece of rope at the bottom of which hangs a pail, or more properly, according to fashion, a basket closely woven. The basket is lowered and filled with water, the man gives it an upward jerk, and the weight of the stone at the other end quickly carries on the impetus, and the water is thus raised to the proper level on the bank.

It is said that the working of the shadoof is hard— whether it be so or not we do not know. Arabs are not wont to give themselves more trouble than they need, but we have wondered sometimes whether the work required by the use of the shadoof is so very much less than would be the labour of lifting the water straight from the river by the aid of a pail and a rope, with no shadoof at all.

On the highly cultivated lands as many as three harvests may be obtained in the year off the same ground. First wheat or barley or lupins are sown ; when that harvest is gathered in, a sowing with millet or indigo takes place; after that has been reaped, the ground is again sown with millet a second time or maize. So fertile is the soil that little labour is required that these great (to English minds) results may be obtained. The growth of crops in Egypt is luxuriant in the extreme.

Very lovely is the appearance of the Cairo gardens in the spring; and though the country can hardly be said to be famed for flowers, still the orange and lemon trees, palms and bananas, acacias and oleanders, pointzettias and aloes, all go to make the scene effective. Marguerites and nasturtiums, geraniums and ageratums, sweet-williams and beautiful roses of all kinds bloom in profusion, but there is a great lack of grass. The houses in Cairo are rendered a picture by the bougainvillea creeper with its hanging blossoms of a deep purplish mauve—so different from the ghastly colour they assume even in hothouses in England.

Palm groves lend a charm to the open country, and their appearance by moonlight is soft and enchanting. Some very pretty wooded walks may be found beyond what is known at Mena as the second village (an annexe of Kafra), where tamarisk trees and palms and prickly pears blend together in a beautiful negligence. The latter plants are often used for hedges to surround the cultivated gardens; awkward, graceless shrubs they are, and yet not without a kind of beauty. Aloes are much cultivated, for there is supposed to be a charm about them; they are grown in tubs, and placed on the housetops, and specially also over graves and tombs.

The birds of Egypt are very beautiful in plumage, if not in song, and abound near Mena—huge brown vultures and falcons, buzzards and kites, which seem to poise themselves in mid-air with no apparent movement of muscle or wing; crows, large and powerfully built, with a grey head piece and a wise and crafty look; lovely white ibises or paddy birds, properly called herons; cream coloured coursers; snipe, and endless quantities of quail; lovely hoopoes, with their knowing look, and green bee-eaters later in the spring; dapper little birds of black and white plumage, which flit from stone to stone, and sweep across the fields; elegant wagtails, and owls pretending to look grave—all these may every day be found. Scavenger birds fulfil a most important function, for they keep the desert perfectly clear of decaying substance. What the vultures leave, the dogs devour, and what they leave, the beetles undermine and bury.

It is curious in the desert to notice how the creatures which pass their life within it are more or less the colour of the sand. Snakes and lizards, and mammals and birds, spiders and beetles, and snails are all of a neutral tint. Once or twice we have been startled to see the sand grouse running along, hardly discernible from the ground; and to notice what was apparently a little lump of sand—but really a beetle—take sudden life, and hurry under a stone. Holes, from which issue forth colonies of ants of considerable size may frequently be found. The long " runs " of these insects often stretch for a great distance, sometimes upwards of twenty-five yards.

CHAPTER XVI.

EVENTS OF INTEREST.

WE remember how on one occasion the height of the Pyramid dawned on us. We were hardly acquainted with its size and appearance, and at first we had thought it by no means so huge as we expected. Turning our gaze there one morning we saw what looked like huge black flies on its surface. We looked again, and found the huge black flies were living human beings. Once we witnessed a strangely incongruous scene. It was New-Year's Eve. The whole number of the hotel waiters had mounted to the summit at midnight to welcome in the New Year. To see the darkness lit up with Bengal lights, and to hear from the top of that monument of antiquity the well-known sounds of " God save the Queen," was an experience we shall never forget.

There was considerable excitement one day in the neighbourhood of Kafra, for a wedding was about to take place, and this would ensure a village fantasia.

There was quite a gathering of women and boys about 3 o'clock. A few men too had come to enjoy the occasion all armed with guns, whether it was according to usual custom or owing to excitement we cannot say but their manner of handling these firearms was

GROUP OF CAMELS.

(By permission, from a photograph by Zangaki.)

somewhat startling to lookers on, unversed in the
innocence of their movements ; for no sooner had they
pointed their guns in one direction than they turned
sharply round, and faced the other way, the guns
remaining pointed as they moved ; after sundry
jumps and continued turning backwards and forwards, they would shoot with a very excellent chance
of hitting somebody. Of course, they assured us the
weapons were only loaded with powder—an excuse
often made with fatal consequences; but as even powder
discharged in our eyes we imagined might be painful,
we withdrew to a respectful distance.

The excitement seemed to be increasing, till at last
the band arrived and enjoyment was at its height.
The band consisted of a by no means tuneful drum,
and three horns of squeaky sound. The effect of the
music, which was not charming, resembled that of a
drum and fife band when all the fifes are cracked,
but for Arab ears the noise had an attraction. The
next business was to prepare a bower for the bride,
which they did by affixing in an upright position
four palm branches to the corners of a square board
placed on the ground, the tops of these branches
being tied together and forming one feathery plume ;
this skeleton tent was now draped with a counterpane
and became a canopy fit for the sacred carpet itself.
The whole thing was tied on to a camel's back, and
into this bower the bride was put for the procession
round the town. A second camel was now brought,
and a huge net was attached to each side of the
saddle ; in one was placed a gaily painted coffin-like
box, containing we were told the trousseau ; while

in the other were placed the bed, and blankets, and sundry pieces of furniture, as well as, no doubt, the frying pan and the inevitable saucepan. These were " all the worldly goods with which one was endowing the other"; but which was the donor and which the recipient we could not quite make out, for the husband buys the wife, and the wife with the money buys the trousseau which she takes to him ; this is the same as saying that the husband buys the trousseau, and gets the wife for nothing.

There was a great shouting made by the boys to cheer everybody up as the procession started to go round the village. The men with the fire-arms led the way, pausing at times, and while jumping and dancing fired off the guns ; other men fought with sticks or pretended to do so, for we never saw them hit each other : then came the camels with the bride, who all the time in her bower was receiving a fearful jolting : after these followed the women friends and many young girls. Noise, and clamour, and shrieks were heard on every side, and we were told that this is a great opportunity for the lads to select their future wives. As in England so in Egypt, one wedding leads to many more. At last the procession arrived at the bridegroom's house, the bride entered it and remained ; the bridegroom himself was far away feasting in the house of a friend ; the betrothal and the dowry had of course been arranged long before ; at night in solemn procession he would return to his home, and there receive his bride from the hand of her friends.

One afternoon while walking from the Sphinx on to

the plain below, a great noise assailed our ears. In the village hard by a tribal feud was evidently in progress, for from all quarters people were hurrying with excited cries and there was a veritable gathering of the clans. Men dropped their outer cloaks for the women to carry home, and brandishing thick sticks (which seemed as if by miracle to be forthcoming) rushed to the fray. What the exact cause of the quarrel was we never made out; but in the babel of conflicting tongues we thought we understood that a man from a neighbouring village had disputed over money with one living at Kafra. A quarrel ensued; one banged the other, and somebody's head was broken.' Blood had been drawn, which was a serious fact. Representatives came to defend their champion's rights, all armed with " broom-sticks," and making a fearful row. They clashed each others' sticks; they seized each others' limbs, and held them tight; their faces bore every mark of passion, but the chief method of warfare seemed to consist in banging each others' clothes. It was a great disturbance; dust in large quantities was thrown in the air; women flew to the scene, uttering cries of woe.* They joined their hands, and threw them far behind their heads; then brought them sharply forward while gradually parting them, to signify that the broil must cease. All were screaming to their hearts' content. At times a fight did seem imminent, but the blows always descended on ample skirts, and no one was badly hit. We could

* These cries sounded to us like hoch! hoch! possibly they may have been the familiar ul! ul!

not refrain from thinking them a very poor lot of cowards, and we felt one English boxer would have put the whole of them to the rout.

At last the men of the farther village began to depart, and the shêkhs ordered their own men to "move on"; but the excitement still kept up. A man standing by himself who, we had noticed, had taken no part in the melée, would seem suddenly inspired with a talking mania, and would begin narrating the whole thing to the rest, who took no notice of what he said—then another some way off would take up the parable, and so on from time to time. No one paid the slightest heed, but still they continued to give their version of the affair. They reminded us of old hens cackling out a story when the fowl-roost has been disturbed. The finish of this instructive and entertaining episode was that we were called on to give evidence as witnesses. Considering that we had longed for blows instead of mere bravado, and had failed to see any delivered, and that the distinctive characteristics of one Arab were to us exactly like those of another, we declined to occupy the invidious position of taking a side in a possibly none too sweet native tribunal. Certainly if somewhat against their wish, the officials were wise in not continuing to demand our testimony, which could have in no way helped to elucidate the rights and wrongs of the case, but only to condemn everybody all round. Eventually things quieted down, and we heard no more. For the future, if we saw even the prospect of any quarrel impending in any of the villages, important business would immediately summon us away; for "witnessing" under such circumstances may be a highly unpleasant task.

One afternoon a small crowd of boys were watching some air balloons being sent off near the Pyramids. A tiny member of their number suddenly declared the stirrup had been stolen from his donkey, and a prolonged howling and whining began. He laid the charge of theft against a person or persons unknown, but as an act of precaution seized the bridle of the nearest camel, and stuck to it like grim death. The sight of this small specimen of humanity flooded in tears of abject grief at the loss of his stirrup, quietly appropriating a camel which was many times his own size, until his stirrup should be restored, was comic in the extreme. We tried the case, but could prove nothing. At last the stirrup was produced discovered in a neighbouring hole. Hereupon the small boy attacked the supposed culprit ; then the elder brothers on each side took part in the fray and there was a row, sticks being freely used. One got a knock on the head and fainted. He was restored by water being dashed on his face. When brought to, he promptly attacked the man who had the kindness to revive him. A general melée now began, and the shèkhs had to be summoned.

One day the Arab gardener was quietly at work by the hotel, and had placed his shoes close by him on the path. There was a sudden thud, and one of the shoes jumped upward in the air. In dire astonishment the Arab picked it up and looked it round. Here was an evil spirit clearly at work. By the beard of the Prophet ! the shoe was possessed ! After considerable inspection, the gardener in consternation resumed his work, as no explanation seemed at hand. Yet another minute, and there was another thud, and the second shoe flew up in the air. "Allah! Allah!" cried the excited man. Here was a miracle indeed. Other Arabs were summoned to witness the magic shoes, and quite a party assembled to chatter, and wonder, and discuss. The good man doubtless believes to this day that some spirit possessed those shoes. It was a bullet in each case, accurately aimed from an air-gun, and shot from a window of the hotel by a friend of ours, which by extreme good luck took such unerring effect. Behind the shutters he was roaring with laughter, at the unwonted result which had attended his piece of innocent fun.

We recall how, on an occasion, it had entered the mind of one, who was never so happy as when delighting children, to have for the Arab boys and girls a downright good English school treat. Prizes of all kinds were purchased from Cairo, and a goodly array of young people—upwards of 300—were invited. The time drew on, and only 50 had appeared. In dismay scouts were sent round to the neighbouring villages, to give a second invitation. The answer came back that, as the electric light in the hotel had failed for a little while the night before, none of the mothers would let the children come, for they felt sure our aim was to get hold of a boy for sacrifice, whereby to appease the angry and offended deity, who had caused the light to fail. The parents of those who did attend, knew us better, and therefore feared less the clandestine and uncanny design.

For the children who were there the races seemed to have little attraction ; the only aim they had was to seize all the prizes they could, and it was a matter of amazement to the boys that anything should be done for the girls. Egyptian children have a lot to learn, before they will manifest the cheerful brightness and common sense, the submission to rules, and general " esprit de corps," which, in most cases, would be the distinctive characteristics of English children on a like occasion.

One of the sportsmen residing in the hotel, on one occasion killed at close quarters a fine specimen of the wild cat or lynx ; the fur showed that the animal had been shot close at hand ; friends jokingly hinted it was a large tame cat, decked with a blue ribbon and bell, which the slayer had cruelly enticed by honied words. Meanwhile the skin was being dried ; unfortunately from insufficient curing the tail took to doing badly, and had to be destroyed. We suggested as a substitute, a spiral lamp-brush— but whether or not our idea was followed out, we do not know.

On another occasion a party went forth at dusk, to shoot jackals—animals which are often to be seen in the neighbourhood. The sun had set, and in the rapidly increasing darkness there appeared to be some game worth shooting close at hand. The prize was duly stalked and shot, and proved to be what was thought a small specimen of the genus *wild boar*. It was solemnly borne home in triumph on the shoulders of the shikari. When nearing home the party encountered some of the Arab servants of the hotel eagerly looking for something. The object of their search proved to be one little stray tame pig, which had been purchased for the yard, and had just managed to escape. The last of this joke was not heard for some days.

CHAPTER XVII

EXCURSIONS AND EXPEDITIONS.

RIDES in the desert on camel-back are always exhilarating. They are still more enjoyed when once the habit has been learned of moving as the camels move and of offering no resistance to the swaying to and fro which their ambling slouch causes the rider to undergo. Very romantic do the strange beasts look as they move quietly along saddled with a wealth of many coloured trappings.

The mounting itself is an easy matter as they lie upon the ground with their long unwieldy necks stretched out flat on the sand ; but then comes the tug of war during which it is well to hold tight ; all the while you are settling yourself, as you think, comfortably, the camel is making a noisy, unmusical, groaning complaint at the irony of life which compels him to thus minister to the carrying of man ; he is at all times a supercilious looking creature, unloving and unloved, and when about to be made to work, puts on a still more unpleasant expression ; you may be his master for the time, but he will take the pride out of you as much as he can. First his hind legs are partly raised, and you are nearly pitched forward ; then the raising of his forelegs reverses the process, and you are nearly pitched backwards ; there is still one more prolonged and jerky movement to straighten the hind and front legs, during which you have a renewed inclination to fall ; if you have clung on through all this, you are safe for a time, but the jolting will cause you some excitement for the first half-mile. The reversing of this process, when he is arranging himself on the ground for you to dismount is even more distasteful to endure.

The desert is wide, and a ride may be taken in any direction, the camel's feet being admirably suited to the sand. A pleasant journey may also be made to the Petrified Forest, and to some other places of interest.

A very enjoyable expedition may be made to the ruined Pyramid of Aboo-roash. The way is along the desert edge to the north. The atmosphere, as usual, is deliciously fresh, and the sense of the invigorating air is very charming. Flocks of flamingoes may be seen sometimes whirling up from the road, dangling their long legs ; and at periods of the year the carpet of flowers is very gay, specially when the purple orchids are in bloom. After a long stretch of sand a turn to the left is made, and the ascent of the hill is begun. There is nothing very striking about the road until the defile, which leads to the top of the cliff, is reached. It is interesting to notice here what a lot of vegetation exists ; it is difficult to tell how anything green can find moisture ; but here on the glaring arid sand many a plant seems to luxuriate, and on every plant may be discovered several snails ; in addition to others, the ice plant grows in abundance, and is a sight of joy to the camel, with its juicy succulent stems full of watery sap. We pass onward by huge boulders and awkward looking rocks until we reach the top of the hill.

The plateau here is higher, and the view from the summit is lovely, stretching far in every direction ; far away to the north we gaze, and imagine the position of Alexandria, where the ships lie which, we trust, will shortly bear us back to home and friends ; nearer at hand is the Barrage, the towers of which are plainly visible ; from that, right away to the south, winds a blue streak, which we know to be the river Nile ; for a long way we can trace its course, beneath the pink hills of Mokattam ; far away in front of us lies Cairo itself, looking from this position a town of very considerable size, overtopped by the frowning citadel, where the white mosque minarets stand clearly out against the blue background of sky.

We get from here a most excellent view of the whole desert ; and the pyramids of Gizeh, as if conscious of their superior size, form an effective spectacle on the sand ; the forms of those at Abooseer and Dashoor loom far away in the distance. Leading up to the plateau are the remains of the causeway, by which the stones were brought for the pyramid, which is now a mere ruin ; the foundations, which still remain, are well and solidly made, and this pyramid on its elevated site must once have been a very striking object. Immediately below the cliff is the large straggling palm grove which enriches the scene, and forms a pleasing foreground to the mud villages which lie beyond. Around us on all sides are rubbish heaps, and here in greater abun-

dance than anywhere else in the neighbourhood may
be found those small pieces of red pottery (like egg
cups and saucers) which some affirm to be of Roman
date, but others ascribe to far more ancient times.

There is little shade at Aboo-roash, and after
lunch, taken very awkwardly under such shelter
from the sun's rays as might be obtained, after one
more look at the glorious view, we summoned our
guides, gave backsheesh to the boys, who had done
certain kindnesses for us, and returned. A race home
over the desert in sand carts is not without its
amusement, provided the temper of the mules is such
as to make them willing to go fairly fast.

Another charming ride may be made through the
palm groves beyond the race course. Monday is a
favourite day for this excursion, when at the village of
Kerdasa in the palm woods a weekly fair is held.
Those who go to see the ways of the country will not
be disappointed, but they must be prepared at the fair
itself to find a fearful state of dirt. Donkeys can
well stand this trip, and very delightful it is to pass
through the groves of palms, past tomato plantations
and gardens which are being carefully irrigated and
tilled ; the fitful shadows of the waving branches
fall prettily upon the sand ; birds chatter in the trees,
and flit across the path ; the air is laden with scent,
and with the hum of bees ; groups of peasants pass
or meet us on their way to or from the fair, with
their camels and donkeys laden with stores ; villagers
are attending to their sakiehs, or working their
shadoofs.

Arrived at the village, we dismount, and our guide

A PALM GROVE.

(By permission, from a photograph by Zangaki.)

conducts us to the densely crowded square, where visitors must not mind somewhat of a crush among people who are none too clean. Business of all kinds is going on. Men are selling, bartering, haggling, and cheating ; camels are being clipped, and buffaloes slaughtered ; all kinds of beasts are for sale ; barbers are shaving Arab faces, and cropping Arab heads ; shoemakers, tailors, butchers, saddlers, basket makers, bakers, public writers, all are at work ; everybody is chattering, and making a dust, but all are in a good temper. We wish we were not quite such *raræ aves ;* we should then possibly be surrounded less closely, but as we are foreigners, nothing will keep the people off. All things that the villagers use can be purchased here ; grain of all kinds, and pretty-looking piles of seed of many colours, placed in open baskets ; sugar cane and tomatoes ; shoes and clothes ; toys and house utensils ; furniture and ornaments ; food and provender ; jewelry and gaudily marked Manchester goods ; pipes and tobacco—all may be bought here. The whole scene is indeed a moving panorama ; but it was noisy, dusty, and very hot, and we were not sorry once again to mount our donkeys, and get into purer air, under the shade of the spreading palms. We have often purchased dresses and nick-nacks of many kinds, but the thing which has perhaps given most amusement to our English friends is a real Egyptian doll, which must be seen to be realized.

CHAPTER XVIII.

FOR the excursion to Sakkarah still weather is a necessity, for it is the outing of a day. No anxiety need be experienced on the score of rain, for that may be said never to come ; but there are sure to be drawbacks in every land, and a high boisterous wind blows the sand with such force from the desert that to be out in the piteous blast is most trying to eyes, nose, and face. On the few days in the winter, when these sand storms prevail the wisest plan is to remain in the house, for the whole air becomes like a thin sandy fog, and the outlook appears miserable indeed.

We remember how once, when out for this particular excursion, we had started on a morning of cloudless beauty, and the outward journey was delightful. While at Sakkarah, however, a gale arose, and the sand blew everywhere in a thick cloud. So stinging was the effect of it during that long drive home that we could hardly see to guide the mule. We sorely longed for veils, and for some days our faces were painfully sore.

For journeys along the edge of the desert the hotel supplies capital little carts with broad-tired wheels which refuse to sink in even on the soft sand. The lunch is generally sent on with a shikari on a camel. We recommend the hire of these sand carts in preference to donkeys, for the ride there and back for them is a long and tiring one. The road is not very clearly delineated, nor is the scenery as we pass very striking, though birds and flowers of all kinds gladden the way. The fascination of the trip lies in the wonderful tonic of the air and in the glorious weather which brightens everything. After an hour and a half's ride we reach the pyramids of Abooseer ; then after a further long stretch through the hills of sand we reach the old tumble-down hovel euphemistically called " the house " of the late M. Mariette, the great excavator, and know that we have come to our journey's end.

The verandah—if such it can be called—of the house has the advantage of being cool ; but of all the dreary localities that we have ever set eyes on this strikes us as one of the worst. M. Mariette must indeed have been enamoured with the prospect of the buried treasure around to live long in this forsaken spot. Considering the number of tourists who come here from day to day we have sometimes thought the authorities might provide a decent table and a few chairs that might be trusted to bear a human weight, let alone many other small improvements which might so easily be made ; but Egypt is Egypt, and the state of hopeless discomfort there will no doubt for years remain. One of the custodians of the house possessed the largest nose we ever had the sadness to see disfiguring a human face ; but the good old soul was unconscious of his unprepossessing

I

appearance. Time on days such as these quickly goes,
and we thought it well at once to see the
Serapeum or burying place of the Apis bulls. He
who enters here must be prepared for a hot and
still, but by no means stifling atmosphere : we were
told it was the mean temperature of Egypt ; if so, the
summer heat must be very great. The entry is
made by a door below the level of the ground ; and
by means of a few sandstorms all trace of the place
might be quickly covered up again. We could not
help thinking how much may lie hidden in the desert
since traces of large erections can be so quickly buried
in. On entering we found ourselves at the beginning
of a series of long tunnels hollowed out of the rock,
and somewhere about fifteen feet in height. On either
side of these tunnels are further large chambers also
hollowed out of the rock like side chapels in a great
cathedral ; in these chambers, and filling up the
greater part of them, are huge granite sarcophagi,
speaking roughly about twelve feet square, of which
some are provided with massive lids ; in these once
reposed the mummied remains of the sacred bulls.
All this labour and trouble was taken for the carcases
of kine ; and some twenty-five of these sculptured
cenotaphs still remain each in their separate rock-cut
home, and each cut out of a solid block of granite.
How the Egyptians ever moved these huge masses
through the narrow and by no means lofty corridors
seems a marvel ; but then we are in Egypt, and the
inhabitants of former times when they did things
did them well, for they worshipped Deity of
course under these animal forms ; but even with that

fact before us the whole conception left a strange impression of amazement on our minds, and we were glad to gain once more the outer air and to leave this sepulchral gloom, where all had seemed shadowy and mysterious.

We returned to the house for lunch. The faithful Arab had prepared all for us, and it was a treat to assuage hunger and thirst. The soda water and the claret had been packed in a lead-lined box, to which the waiter had thoughtlessly added two huge lumps of ice. The jolting of the camel had caused a breakage, and we found a curious mixture of a ready-made claret cup covered with a sea-like foam. However we had to be thankful for small mercies, and we were glad to drink the concoction, for the heat was excessive ; and we can recall now the kind of suffused glow that some of the ladies' countenances presented, for extreme heat or cold does not improve complexions. We shortly started for the tomb of Ti, which is of course much older than, and very different from, the Mausoleum of the Bulls, and dates back to the Pyramid times. The tomb is a building with several rooms of no very large dimensions ; but the interest of the place consists in the elaborate, coloured, and sculptured pictures of life under every form and condition well raised in clear relief on the walls of the chambers. As on the day when they were made they can be clearly deciphered, and we felt that as we gazed we might be living in ancient Egypt, amid all the strange, quaintly represented customs so distinctly here pourtrayed and chiselled. There are representa-tions of religious ceremonies, of fishing, and shooting, and cooking; of sheep and oxen, camels and asses, geese and alligators; every trade and every profession, every rank and station of life as it was 6,000 years ago is before us as we look. Accurately and artistically is the whole thing done, true indeed to life. There is one further interesting spot to notice, the burying place of Ti himself; far away from all the lavishly decorated rooms, put where few would think of looking, in an odd corner at the end of a long tunnel which led down from the entrance chamber into the very heart of the rock, some thirty feet or so—there in solemn state the body of Ti was laid. When the coffin was placed *in situ* the whole approach was completely filled in, and the entrance closed with level masonry; the existence of the passage was carefully concealed in order that the mummied body might rest in peace until the soul returned to the clay. This story of desired secrecy and repose for the bodies of their dead is a common one in Egypt; but in nearly all cases their tombs have been rifled and disturbed. The absolute contempt for the wishes of the dead is a sad part of all excavation.

One new tomb has recently been brought to light, that of Khabil. It is full of hieroglyphs and is larger by far than that of Ti, and with less painting, but otherwise very similar, although possessing many more rooms. The glory of this newly excavated place is the statue of the founder, which remains intact in its proper place, and has *not yet* been moved to any museum; it is a fine, imposing statue dressed according to the fashion of the day, and painted marvellously well. In the niche behind we noticed the pattern of the decoration was of bars of white and yellow ; these colours one may see still stamped on many of the fabrics which are sold in the bazaars of to-day.

A further interesting visit may be made to the Step Pyramid of Oonephes,—possibly an erection of earlier date than that of Cheops. Had we had time we might have prolonged our ride to Memphis, once the royal abode of the kings ; now all that remains is some heaps of rubbish and the remnants of a huge statue which lies flat upon the ground, and forms another instance of Egypt's departed glory.

The sun was slowly westering, and we hastened to return ; the lunch camel having already gone on before. Quickly we took our seats, and started for home ; from the village by the way bright-eyed boys ran out and offered a drink of water from their cool jars ; we refused, for we knew not whence the water had been drawn, but the cheerful manners of the little lads amused us much. The drive home in the warm evening was very pleasant, and we arrived none too tired, satisfied in feeling that we had gone through a most instructive day.

CHAPTER XIX.

SHOOTING IN EGYPT.

SNIPE-SHOOTING in Egypt commences early in November, and ends in March,—December and January being the best months. The sport varies both in Upper and Lower Egypt with the amount of water that is on the land at the time, and the season varies according to the height of the Nile,—a season with a high Nile being generally the best. This sport is never very good in the immediate neighbourhood of Mena, but five to ten brace a day, and possibly more may be ordinarily obtained ; as a criterion, we may mention that in short excursions of three hours at a time we have shot 50 couple in ten outings round the hotel, during December and January.

Excursions can however be made from Mena to more or less distant shooting grounds.* Excellent sport can be obtained at Tel-el-Kebir, Kafr-Shekh, the Fayûm, the Delta, and that part of the Nile that lies between Minieh and Esneh. Atfeh is also very good, and there are some well stocked marshes near Bemba. Splendid duck-shooting can be obtained on Lake Menzaleh, and Lakes Boorlos

---

* We are indebted for many hints on distant shooting grounds to the various letters, &c., which have appeared in "The Field" from time to time during the last few years.

A DAHABEAH.

and Etko near the coast, where immense numbers of water-fowl congregate, including ducks of all species, and the white fronted goose; but in consequence of the latter being difficult of approach a boat is necessary for this kind of shooting. Amongst the waders the spur-winged plover, the painted snipe, the white heron (mistaken often for the sacred ibis), and the pelican are the most interesting and numerous.* The wet marshy ground from Tel-el-Kebir to Mahsameh is as good as any place in Egypt for snipe and duck; while later in the season when the Nile water has subsided and left the inland places dry, Damietta and Shirbin are good, as well as the neighbourhood of Aboo-homus, about 30 miles from Alexandria; but owing to the vicinity of the city, these latter places are apt to be much shot over, and sport may be disappointing; excellent duck shooting can also be obtained all through the winter months on the Nile Delta, near Rosetta and Damietta, but for this a boat in which to live is necessary.

The great difficulty which the sportsman everywhere has to contend against in Egypt, is the entire absence of any but the most wretched accommodation. For the Nile, nothing can exceed the comfort of a dahabeah, which is a sort o house-boat, drawing only a few feet of water and carrying a main and mizen mast.† Its progress is

---

* In Lake Menzaleh and the Nile, fish are plentiful.

† All arrangements for the hire of one of these boats can be made through Messrs. T. Cook & Son, in Cairo. The Nile trip can be done comfortably in about three months, and costs for two persons from £300 to £400 inclusive.

slow as it is mostly dependent on the wind, and owing to the very little ballast it takes, it cannot carry much sail, if the wind be strong. Numerous varieties of duck and aquatic birds frequent the Nile in winter, and afford excellent sport ; amongst them we may mention the wild duck, the pochard, the teal, the sheldrake, the pintail, and the shoveller.

Up the Nile, at Luxor, duck and snipe are found in December and January in the marshy ground south of the town ; while in the canals and cuttings from the Nile duck and teal are sometimes plentiful ; quail shooting, too, in March and April can be enjoyed by those staying in the town, as well as by those on dahabeahs on the Nile. Messrs. T. Cook and Son offer every facility to sportsmen going up on their river boats, making no charge for guns and ammunition if taken by passengers. Cartridges should be declared, however, that they may be put into a safe place ; and firearms are not allowed to be used from the deck.

"The shooting in the neighbourhood of Suakin consists of quail, bustard, common gazelle, hares and sandgrouse. At Assouan, and Wady-Halfa there is very little shooting to be had, what there is, consists of sandgrouse, plover, and gazelle." *

For land expeditions our advice to all is to camp out ; a trustworthy shikari can be engaged at Mena or at Cairo, who will supply everything essential for a shooting expedition, such as tents, food and transport for about 30s. a day per person. No climate can excel that of Egypt for camping out in, and it is curious why

* Field 1890.

sportsmen do not avail themselves more of this mode of life; for the cost would hardly, if at all, exceed that of hotel life in Cairo with its incidental expenses. February and March, would be the best months as by then the ground would be more or less dry owing to the subsidence of the Nile.

As regards the clothing most suitable for shooting in Egypt, our advice is to wear always woollen underclothing next the skin, and a flannel shirt, and to bring out from England a suit of ordinary shooting clothes made of some light but warm woollen texture, also a suit of "kakee" which will wash, and so prove very serviceable. For head covering we have found nothing better than a "terai" hat, which can be worn double or single according to the month of the year and heat of the sun. It is useless to try and keep out the water from one's boots; but what we found far more disagreeable than wet is the very heavy and tenacious thick black mud, which is present in all places where snipe are found, and which makes the "going" very heavy. This as a rule gets into the insides of one's boots and stockings; by way of preventing this, we devised two years ago, a pair of shooting boots* with stout soles and nails, and with uppers of strong brown canvas, which stretch in one piece like a "Wellington" to below the knee, where they can be tightened to the leg with a strap and buckle, but are open up the front for a certain distance for lacing; the opening being closed as well with a large soft tongue sewn firmly to the side to prevent any mud from entering; a toe-cap of

* Commonly known as the "Field boot pattern."

leather and cross band of the same material across the foot, as in cricketing shoes, gives the necessary strength. These boots before being taken off are easily washed clean of mud as soon as the shooting is over, and in drying they never shrink. A sportsman provided with two pairs would find them invaluable in Egypt.

In the months of December and January, when the Nile has so far subsided as to leave numerous little lakes and canals along the sides of the dykes, the sportsman will find these waters frequented by large numbers of aquatic birds, and good sport can be obtained among them as well as an agreeable ride at the same time. Sandgrouse (called by the natives " Kata" from their cry), red-legged partridges and cream-coloured coursers are also found at times in great numbers along the edge of the desert in February and March, and can be easily stalked if the rider has his gun with him ; while vultures, of which there are several of the naked-necked species, and of the aquiline variety, together with a stray wolf, offer fine marks for the rifleman. For this purpose he should be provided with some sort of sling* for carrying his gun on horseback.

We may mention that close to Mena House, amongst the rocks at the back of the Pyramids, two or three species of the genus *canis* may be found, *i.e.*, the fox, the jackal, and the Egyptian wolf (canis Sinensis). The latter have on different occasions given good sport when found in the open by the horseman out for his

---

* That invented by Messrs. Bland and Co. for this purpose is excellent.

early morning or evening ride. Should he happen to have his gun with him and to be provided with one of Bland's slings he can, when mounted on one of the Mena House arabs, have an exciting chase, and come home probably with the brush. This has been done more than once, as readers in the *Field* will have noticed ; † only last winter a fine specimen was ridden down and speared, after an exciting half-hour's gallop in the desert, by three officers stationed in Cairo. To those who care for the sport of jackal shooting Mena affords the best opportunity. They frequent the rocks and large loose stones of the smaller pyramids, and in the evening prowl around for food ; a worn out donkey or other sickly animal is shot and left near their lair, and a watch is kept ; in a short time one or more jackals, attracted by the smell, put in an appearance, and may as a rule be bagged. The arab shikaris at Mena are well used to this kind of sport.

The sport " par excellence," for which Mena is justly celebrated, is quail shooting. These small game birds, which belong to the genus *coternix* are migratory by nature, and arrive in the neighbourhood of Cairo from the south, in their passage to their northern breeding grounds, in immense quantities in the months of March and April ; and return in even larger numbers in September from Europe. The male bird is easily distinguished by the reddish or dark-brown bands running down each side of the

† They will find in the number for April 18th, 1894, a graphic account of successful rides by the late Sir Victor Brooke and Mr. R. H. Clarke.

throat ; in the hen bird these marks are absent, and
the breast is spotted like a thrush ; when put up,
they seldom fly far, and it is exceedingly difficult to
make them take the wing a second time. They are
the same birds as are mentioned in " Exodus " as
having supplied food to the Israelites in the wilder-
ness. The American quail, and the button quail of
India and the Malay archipelago belong to distinct
families.

The part of the Nile valley between Mena and Cairo,
a stretch of some nine miles of flat but diversified
ground, cultivated with birsin, clover, wheat, trefoil, and
beans, and beautified with a profusion of flowers—
the poppy, the clover, the lupin, and the flax—in
March and April teems with quail. They are of a
rich brown plumage, with darker markings, very like
those of the snipe, and in appearance and size like a
diminutive partridge ; they afford excellent sport and
splendid practice to the old and young shot, but
are by no means so easy to kill as is generally
supposed, for no two birds fly alike, especially on a
windy day. They usually come down from Upper
Egypt with the first Khamseen, or hot wind, which
generally blows for two consecutive days on a few
occasions in the months of March and April ; on
arrival they are in a very exhausted and poor
condition, and afford an easy mark to the sportsman ;
but after a rest for a week or two on the rich feeding
ground round the hotel they fatten, and are then
quick on the wing. Nothing can be more pleasant or
invigorating than a day amongst the quail ; leaving
the hotel at 9.30 after breakfast, and provided with

lunch which is put up by the hotel free, and supplied
with whatever drinkables we may choose to order, a
start is made; our shikari who has chosen for us
four or six small boys as beaters, meets us on the
hotel steps; anywhere within a quarter of a mile
from the hotel birds may be found; but although we
have now for three seasons been out quail shooting,
we have not yet fully learned their habits, or the
reason why on some days they should be in the
wheat, while on others mostly in the clover or lupin.
After arrival on the ground a line is formed, with the
'guns' placed at convenient distances between the
beaters; an advance is made through the standing
crops, either clover fields or lupin patches, the
shikari and beaters meanwhile making a peculiar
noise in regular and rhythmical time as they advance;
as a rule, the birds lie very close and are often passed
over; when they rise they do so within a few feet of
the beaters. Their flight is very quick and, as a rule,
very low and straight, but sometimes with a twisting
motion; and if there is any wind blowing at the
time, they make a very difficult shot, though forty to
fifty brace may easily be killed in a day. There
is generally a breeze coming from the north,
rendering the air deliciously bracing and invigorating,
while above is the more or less cloudless blue
canopy of heaven; the country round presents a
lovely and animated appearance; butterflies and
bees fly in every direction; the ground is carpeted
with flowers, and the air is full of the twitter of the
linnet, the bee-eater, the hoopoe, and the sweet song of
the lark; birds of prey are by no means absent, ready

at a moment's notice to pounce on the wounded quail
and carry him off before the sportsman's eyes,—an
incident which has happened to us on several
occasions.* †

* Among these birds the common buzzard, the moor harrier, and
two kinds of hawk are indigenous.

† The Egyptian Government has a monopoly of the sale of all kinds
of gunpowder, and protects itself by imposing a very heavy duty on
the importation of loaded cartridges, making the cost of these when
delivered about 100 per cent. above the cost of them at home.
Excellent cartridges and gunpowder can be obtained in Cairo at the
establishment of M. Bajocci at the following prices :—

CENTRAL FIRE CARTRIDGES (12 BORE.)

Loaded in England by ELEY BROS.

Brown	...	...	...	...	...	...	Fr. 20 a hundred.
Blue ...	...	...	...	...	..	...	,, 21 do.
Green	...	...	...	...	...	...	,. 22 do.
Schultze	...	...	..	...	...	...	,, 24 do.

GUNPOWDER.

Ordinary...	...	...	...	Fr. 1.80 p. pound.	
F ...	...	...	...	...	,, 2.40	do.
FFF	...	...	...	...	,, 3.—	do.
FFF	...	...	...	...	,, 3.60	do.	in canisters.
TP	...	...	...	...	,, 4.45	do.	do.
Diamond	...	...	...	,, 5.90	do.	do.
Treble Strong ...	...	...	,, 5.90	do.	do.

A cheap and easy method is to send out empty cartridge
cases with sufficient wads, shot, and loading apparatus for
them, and to buy powder in Cairo. This saves the heavy
duty exacted on their importation into Egypt, and also the
difficulty experienced in getting a ship to carry loaded cartridges,
which only the small Mediterranean coasting boats will do. As a rule,
it is advisable to allow six weeks at least for the transport out, as the
delays on the way and at Alexandria are very tedious. The size of

shot most suitable is No. 8 for snipe and quail, and a smaller quantity of No. 4 for duck, &c. Messrs. Perreaux and Co., 5, Jeffrey's Sq., St. Mary Axe, London, E.C., will undertake all the shipping, and their agents in Alexandria save all trouble to sportsmen by clearing and forwarding everything to its destination with all expedition and regularity.‡

‡ Since the above was written the Minister of War has prohibited the importation of loaded cartridges into Egypt. 1894.

CHAPTER XX

THE SPHINX BY MOONLIGHT.

FOR once unwonted energy seized us, and we determined to see the Sphinx amid surroundings which the guide books praise. The moon was at its full, and after dinner we donned once more our dusty boots, put on some extra wraps, and sallied forth. The night was soft and still, and the moonlight shed its gentle restfulness around. Far off might be heard the primitive love-song of a donkey, and the barking of many dogs guarding, as they imagined, the rights of hearth and home. Nearer at hand was plainly audible the musical vibrating tenor croak of countless frogs, carrying on their courtship in reed-lined ponds close by. An occasional owl's hoot lent mystery to the quiet—otherwise all was still. Slowly we began to mount the hill. From beside the wall that lines the road, one after another dusky Arab figure rose up silently and unexpectedly, ever on the alert for earning an honest or dishonest piastre; before we were aware, they stood before us, these strangely blended studies of black and white, with the dark cloak encasing the head and body, and the skirts of the white smock showing beneath. With a simple " Gud nait " they recognized us, and, realizing we had been guided enough, at first were minded to

let us go on our way. Second thoughts induced
them to accompany us with their shambling walk,
as they slowly dragged their slippered feet over the
sand. "You go see Sphinkis—e-e-e-h-h-h?" they
asked; the latter word is a constantly used interro-
gative; it begins on a low note, and finishes four
tones higher up. It was not all pleasure to walk
along the Pyramid plateau by night; for an
occasional boulder that the surrounding deep shadows
had hidden, made us remember we had a toe, and
there was an unpleasant sense of dust gathering on
skirts and trousers, and the ladies complained of the
cold. The walk was tiring, too, and we wondered
whether the sage who said, "After supper walk a
mile," ever tried to go to the Sphinx by moonlight;
had he done so, we doubt if his recipe for health
would have been handed down to posterity. Tall,
weird, rolling figures loomed in the faint light some
way before us, and we wondered whether a bit of the
Pyramid has got a fit of sleep walking; chattering
voices struck our ears; we gathered that it was a party of
French people on camels, who were returning from
seeing what we were bent upon viewing; the strange,
awe-inspiring surroundings went no way towards
checking that exuberant flow of language which a
Frenchman loves. We congratulated ourselves that we
could be silent at times. More Arabs rose up apparently
out of the earth, and interested themselves in our inten-
tions. Here a small party of them were seated quietly in
a circle on the ground, happy in their contentedness;
talking, perhaps, about the coming marriage of one of
their number, or bewailing the fact that they had

that day charged only three times what they ought.
Never can they leave the Pyramids alone, for then,
perchance, some mis-guided traveller might see the
wonders without their aid and would be no worse off.
In all its grandeur the Pyramid of Cheops faced us,
with its front in darkest shadow; we left it on the
right, and passed round it ; at last we began to
descend ; the road was rougher than when we started,
but we were nearing now the great ugly rough-cut
rock that had been made by human hands to look
something like a human-headed beast crouching in
the sand. A few more steps, and we gazed upon the
face which has inspired past generations of men with
horror, and will be a curiosity to thousands still
unborn ; the soft light enabled us to be less
conscious of blemishes, and we could almost forgive
the idiots who broke away the Sphinx's nose, and
small-pox-marked the face, and stole the manly
beard, and thereby made what remains, as people
suppose, the statue of a "she ;" there it was, that
strange monument of a by-gone age, gazing as
it has ever done, for the first rays of the morrow's
dawn.

For once an unusual sight presented itself; to the left
was still the briliant deep blue sky, rich in purest ultra-
marine, across which wondrous fleecy clouds of
creamy white flitted like flocks of sheep on a summer
plain ; but behind the Great Pyramid a storm cloud
of intense darkness gathered, and in the pale half-light
of mystery that wonder of ancient Egypt stood out
against the dark enveloping back-ground beyond.
Gradually the summit was hid in gloom and mist, and

earth seemed joined to sky, and we realised as never before the vastness of that huge tomb of which the top reaches indeed to heaven, and which is a monument produced alike by vanity, and by the needs of the soaring ambition of the soul of man.

For once all seemed real, and we could almost imagine we were standing by the scene in the days of the old monarchy, when these vast tombs that were to be sealed for ever, had just been made. We forgot for the time the rubbish heaps of sand, and the abomination of desolation which is so apparent by day, and the sense of unfitness, and the vulgarity of tourists, and the knowledge that the past can never return. How are the mighty fallen. Here were once buried in solemn state the greatest of earth-born monarchs ; their tombs even then beat the record, and were constructed with enormous toil and labour ; around them, and adjacent to them, in tombs cut out of the solid rock, and of enormous depth and size, were as a high privilege allowed to be buried the bodies of their relations, their ministers, their obsequious retainers and hangers-on ; there they were laid to rest, the mighty, the proud, the learned, the high-born of the world ; now their graves are ruins, and their coffins are gone, for only the dryness of an unusual atmosphere, and the sheltering cover of the drifting sand have brought it about that even these ruins remain. Every valuable that was buried with them has been exposed for sale ; their very bodies have been taken away, and change and decay have laid their mark on all—the glory and the greatness are gone, never to return.

Do their spirits haunt those dishonoured mausoleums and rifled tombs?   Have their souls which were supposed to return to the earth after a thousand years, come back to find the bodies, on the burying and embalming of which their friends bestowed so much care, all broken up and gone?   Are there voices, weird and unearthly, which cry out at night in sorrow for the desecrated shrines in which once reposed imperial bodies, swathed in linen, and soaked in spice, and bedecked with scarab necklets which the Arabs sell, and surrounded by crystal bottles, now all broken and empty but which once contained the tears that fond relations shed?   Are there unnatural visitants which return to the scenes they knew so well, to grieve and mourn and weep?   The Arabs think there are.   If ghosts there be, the Pyramids may well be haunted ; but over them at night enfolds a silence which may most truly be felt, and only the wistful stars gaze down on the scene of departed human greatness and glories that are no more, and on ruins which remind us even now of the cruelty of by-gone days, and of the littleness of human life.

CHAPTER XXI

HOME AGAIN.

WE were at Alexandria once again, and the fresh sea
breeze was pleasant ; after the heat and glare and the
dust of the train the sight of the deep blue waves was
refreshing, and we were glad to get on board. A
small square wooden box which, in a frantic moment,
we had chartered as a recepticle in which to cram
odds and ends, for which no room could be found in
the heavy luggage, greatly exercised the custom house
officials ; they thought it contained dynamite at least ;
the diabolical machine proved to be only a box filled
with native crockery, and at last it was passed.

We shall never forget our departure from Alexandria on a previous memorable occasion ; we were
on the same vessel as Sir Francis Grenfell, then just
called home to high office in England, after holding
for years the post of Sirdar to the Egyptian army.
Owing to his presence on board, our boat received
special honours ; we were saluted and scanned with
interest by the British ironclads, which then lay in
Alexandria Bay ; the yards were manned, the blue-
jackets cheered, and the bands on board played ; very
touching it was in those fair blue waters, in that respect
so unlike the dull grey seas of England, to hear the

well loved strains of " Home, sweet Home," and " Auld Lang Syne."

When the hot weather begins Englishmen have a desire to return to Europe ; Egypt, with its perfect climate, is a pleasant home for the winter months, but England is better still ; for when the spring, with all its beauty, is, they know, brightening the fields, and making glad the heart of man, the old country has for all an irresistible charm.

> Oh ! to be in England
> Now that April's there,
> And whoever wakes in England
> Sees, some morning, unaware,
> That the lowest boughs and the brushwood sheaf
> Round the elm tree bole are in tiny leaf,
> While the chaffinch sings on the orchard bough
> In England—now.
>
> *   •   •   •   •   •
>
> And though the fields look rough with hoary dew,
> All will be gay when noontide wakes anew
> The buttercups, the little children's dower
> —Far brighter than this gaudy melon flower ! *

It is always a joy to be once more in Europe, where our ways are more fully understood. Travel may be a pleasure, but there is no place like home after all. On each occasion we have delighted in our return to England all the more for the bright memories of our sojourn in the land where the sun perpetually shines.

---

* ROBERT BROWNING—" Home thoughts from abroad."

ARRIVAL OF COACH AT MENA HOUSE.

PART II

A FEW PRACTICAL HINTS

FOR INVALIDS

ON THE MAINTENANCE OF HEALTH

IN THE

CLIMATE OF EGYPT.

BY

ARTHUR J. M. BENTLEY, M.D.,

PHYSICIAN TO MENA HOUSE, CAIRO ; EMERITUS PRESIDENT ROYAL MEDICAL
SOCIETY OF EDINBURGH ; FORMERLY COLONIAL SURGEON STRAITS SETTLEMENTS,
MEDICAL ADVISER TO THE JOHORE GOVERNMENT, AND PHYSICIAN TO
H.H. THE SULTAN.

---

*A Paper read before The British Medical Association in
Bristol,* 1894.

London :
SIMPKIN, MARSHALL, HAMILTON, KENT AND CO., LTD.

Contents.

ii.

CONTENTS.

PAGK

The Maintenance of Health in Egypt.

HINTS TO INVALIDS.

SUGGESTIONS TO MEDICAL MEN.

(A Paper read before the British Medical Association, Bristol, 1894.)

PREFACE. In making the few remarks which I am about to offer, I must apologize for any shortcomings on the score of originality. I have spent three winters in Egypt, in the neighbourhood of Cairo, at Mena House, a health resort situated on the edge of the desert, at the foot of the Great Pyramid of Gizeh, and much frequented by invalids ; and I have thought that the experience thus derived may prove of service to such members of my profession as may contemplate sending patients there, as well as to invalids themselves who for the first time leave home in search of improved health.

INFLUENCE OF CLIMATE ON HEALTH. The good effects of a complete climatic change upon certain forms of disease have long been an established fact. But, in order to obtain the full benefit from a residence abroad, not only must cases suitable for

each particular climate be selected, but proper directions for the maintenance of health under the changed
conditions of life must be given. It is from a
failing in this respect that many do not reap full advantage from the change, and in some instances
return home even in a worse condition than when they
left. Thus they bring discredit on the remedy itself,
whereas it is the faulty method used in employ-

CHOICE OF
CLIMATE.
ing it, which is to blame. The
proper choice of a climate is, in the
first place, of vital importance to the invalid; the
physical characters even of different localities vary
immensely, and this fact does not always receive due
consideration when Egypt is selected. Contrast, for
instance, the difference existing between the air of a

IMMENSE
DIFFERENCES
IN THE
CLIMATES OF
UPPER AND
LOWER EGYPT.
crowded town like Cairo and the pure
desert air of Mena, or the almost
absolutely dry air of Luxor or Assouan;
or, again, "the immense differences
existing between the Delta, which is
under the influence of numerous surfaces of water
and cultivated ground, and Upper Egypt, which is
under the influence of the two deserts. In both,
however, the changes of temperature and force of
wind are sudden and great." (Hermann Weber.)

It will thus be seen, in a country presenting in
different localities such variations in climate and
effects, how important a matter it becomes to select
the proper habitat for each particular case, and more
especially when we have to deal with cases of
phthisis.

CLIMATE ADVAN-
TAGES AND
DISADVANTAGES.

Every climate has its disadvantages as well as its advantages, and it is necessary that a patient should be as cognisant of the former, in order, as far as possible, to avoid them, as of the latter, in order to avail himself of them. It is chiefly, I think, due to a want of knowledge of the former that the remedial effects of a climate are at times discredited, and it is to enable invalids to guard themselves against some of these disadvantages that I now draw attention to them.

NECESSITY FOR
REPEATED
CHANGES
OF CLIMATE.

Change of climate, judiciously employed, may and often does, cure a disease when every other form of treatment has failed ; and in cases where it may have, perhaps, only caused amelioration at first, it may, by repeated trials, eventually effect permanent relief ; it is, therefore, not rational to expect always an immediate or rapid cure from any one single change. Chronic maladies of a constitutional character can only be slowly and surely eradicated by successive winterings abroad, and even in these cases only when proper

PRECAUTIONS
AND CAREFUL
REGIMEN ALSO
NECESSARY.

precautions and regimen are observed. Dr. James Clarke, in his work on climate, says in this respect, "that the air, or climate, is often regarded by patients as possessing some specific quality by virtue of which it directly cures the disease. This erroneous view of the matter not unfrequently proves the bane of the invalid, by leading him, in the fulness of his confidence in climate, to neglect other circumstances, an attention to which may be more essential to his

L

recovery than that in which all his hopes are centred ;" and again, "if a patient would reap the full measure of good which his new position places within his reach, he must trust more to himself, and to his own conduct, than to the simple influence of any climate, however genial ; he must adhere strictly to such a mode of living as his case requires ; he must avail himself of all the advantages which the climate possesses, and eschew those disadvantages from which no climate or situation is exempt ; moreover, he must exercise both resolution and patience in prosecuting all this to a successful issue."

CLIMATE OF EGYPT. The climate of Egypt in the winter months may be summed up as dry and tonic, with a season lasting from November to the end of April. It has a mean winter temperature TEMPERATURE. of 62° as compared with Oratava 63°, Madeira 61° 7', Nice 49° 6', Jersey 43° 82', London 41° 7'. In December the maximum temperature out of doors is 69°, in January 67°, February 68°, March 76°, April 84°. The average minimum, 47° for the same months, out of doors, does not concern particularly the invalid, who should be indoors, where the average minimum is 52°, always before sunset. The absolute winter minimum is 33°.

RAINFALL The rainfall in Cairo averages three days each month between December and April; while at Mena House two or three slight showers during the whole time is phenomenal.

The cases that do well from wintering in Egypt are—

1. All forms of chest disease where *rest* is desirable. For such cases the climate of Egypt acts as a charm (Burden Saunderson).

2. All forms of incipient phthisis, where the constitutional disorder preceding the disease is marked and especially where the patients have still plenty of energy left, and are fond of riding in moderation and of a quiet country life.

3. Chronic bronchitis, where the expectoration is more or less abundant, and those with a gouty tendency.

4. Asthma, especially those cases complicated with bronchitis.

5. Gout.

6. Heart disease, if uncomplicated with dropsy.

7. All forms of anæmia and chlorosis.

8. Renal diseases and sufferers from gravel.

9. Convalescents from acute diseases, such as influenza, pleurisy, &c., and in the quiescent forms of chronic affection of the lungs, trachea or bronchi, especially old standing pneumonic conditions following influenza.

10. Atonic forms of dyspepsia.

11. Chronic rheumatism and the milder cases of rheumatoid arthritis.

12. Chorea.

13. Deteriorated health and general break up of the system, following overwork, especially in men, at between 50 and 60 years of age, with gouty tendencies associated with arterial degeneration.

14. "To persons who are either healthy or merely in want of mental rest and recreation, or of healthful occupation ; for instance, persons who are socially or mentally overworked, or who have sustained shocks or disappointments, or who have been exposed to one of the thousand forms of more or less prolonged worry, or who are without profession and occupation, and lack either the power or the inclination to procure a healthy substitute for them. In such persons a winter spent in Egypt may lead to the return of mental energy and bodily health and vigour." (Hermann Weber).

CASES UNSUITED FOR WINTERING IN EGYPT.

The cases which my experience has found to be unsuited for a winter residence in Egypt are—

1. Advanced heart disease, or advanced organic disease of any organ (excepting cases of chronic and extensive lung consolidation, tubercular or otherwise, which are often greatly benefitted).

2. Aortic regurgitation.

3. Locomotor ataxia (the lightning pains seem to be increased by the electrical conditions so frequently present in the desert atmosphere).

4. All forms of skin diseases, especially psoriasis, unless dependent on a gouty diathesis.

5. Insomnia, except when arising from worry or excessive brain work.

6. Some forms of neurosis, and hypochondriacs with a melancholy tendency. To the former, the brilliant sunshine is often irritating ; while to the latter, want of occupation, and the monotony of life in Egypt,

after the novelty of the scene has worn off, is depressing, leading in many cases to "home-sickness."

7. Convalescents from acute diseases, where no actual disease exists, and where exercise is more or less essential for recuperation. For such, the colder and more bracing climate of the Riviera is better. (Burdon Sanderson.)

ADVANTAGES OF THE CLIMATE OF EGYPT. These consist in a moderately uniform, warm, diurnal temperature; in an almost complete absence of rain, and in a bright sunshine mostly all through the winter months, allowing every facility for an outdoor, free, open life. For those who possess sufficient energy and inclination, ample opportunities are afforded for the invigorating exercises of riding and driving, especially the former; whilst for those of a more robust nature, excellent sport will be found available all through the winter, in the immediate vicinity of Mena, where snipe, duck, and quail abound. There is also complete absence at the different health resorts of fog, and of excessive cold anywhere; while outside the large towns there is an absolutely pure desert air. The hotels are luxurious and comfortable, and the food supply good. Vegetables and fish are abundant and fruit unrivalled. There is, besides, a complete absence of typhoid at all the health resorts excepting Cairo itself, and there, there were only three or four cases amongst the English hotel residents during the whole of last winter—any others which may have developed in visitors after they had left Egypt being probably acquired in Alexandria, where the water should not be drunk unless under the advice of residents.

Malaria, also, is unknown at Mena, Luxor, and Assouan, so that the windows of the sleeping apartments, if facing south, can safely be left open, thus ensuring complete ventilation, except in some chest cases, where chill of any kind may be injurious.

DISADVANTAGES   The drawbacks to a winter sojourn in Egypt, and, in fact to anywhere out of England, are—

1. "The injurious habit Egypt shares unfortunately with the Riviera, that invalids do not consult the doctor until they are attacked by serious illness, which they mostly might have escaped from if they had been guided from the beginning by a judicious physician. This matter ought to be impressed by the medical men at home on the invalids whom they send to Egypt." (Hermann Weber.)

2. The ignorance of most invalids as to the nature of the climate to which they resort, and apparently the want of a full appreciation of the real object for which they go abroad, *i.e.*, the restoration of their health.

3. The opportunities which exist everywhere, and which are so readily taken advantage of, more particularly at Cairo, for sight-seeing and social gatherings, with their attendant evils—over-fatigue, over-crowded rooms, and late hours.

4. The distance from home.

5. The occasional cold high winds.

6. The expense.

7. The sudden and sometimes marked fluctuations

ENTRANCE HALL, MENA HOUSE.

of temperature between day and night, and sunshine and shade.

8. The hot Khamseen winds, which commence in February and blow for about two days at a time, accompanied by fine particles of sand suspended in the air, though at other times the country is not dusty.

It is with the object of lessening or obviating altogether the effects of these disadvantages that my paper is chiefly directed.

DIRECTIONS AS TO ROUTE. Nothing has struck me more during my three years' residence at Mena than the ignorance of the great majority of health-seekers, not only as to the nature of the journey they were undertaking when they left home, but also as to where they should go, what they should do on their arrival, or what mode of life generally they should adopt in Egypt.

There is, practically, only *one* port by which an invalid should enter Egypt, and that is Alexandria. The only choice should lie in the route and line of steamers he should elect to travel by. The lines that make Alexandria the port of call are the P. & O., the Messageries Maritimes, the Austrian Lloyd, the Rubbatino, the Papayani, and the Moss Lines.

The P. & O. is that recommended, then the Messageries Maritimes. The Moss and Papayani, both starting from Liverpool, are cheaper, but do not carry a medical officer.

LONG SEA There are two distinct *routes*, one of which I shall call "The Long Sea," where the passenger gets on board at the docks or at Gravesend in the case of the P. & O., and proceeds *via* Gibraltar and Malta to Brindisi. Here he should change into the *direct* P. & O. boat for Alexandria, where he arrives some time in the forenoon three days after leaving Brindisi.

In the other, or "Short Sea" route
II. SHORT SEA. the passenger goes by *rail* from London to Brindisi, where he embarks in the same P. & O. direct boat to Alexandria.

There is also a P. & O. direct service to Alexandria from Naples. This has a shorter land journey from London, and correspondingly longer sea passage. It has, however, the great advantage of the Brindisi route, in having Alexandria as its port of disembarkation, which is the chief thing for the invalid to bear in mind. The Messageries Maritimes line of steamers, from Marseilles to Alexandria, are convenient for some. They leave Marseilles every fortnight, and take five days to reach Alexandria, arriving there always in the forenoon. The land journey in this case is only 32 hours.

The former, or "Long Sea" route, is
LONG SEA. strongly recommended to all who like the sea, and who are not afraid of a little sea-sickness. Those who travel by it should sleep on board in flannel, and between the blankets, using no sheets, until the warm weather is reached at Gibraltar or Malta. They usually arrive much benefitted in health by the voyage, and in this way the longer journey may be converted into a positive advantage. They should always tranship at Brindisi

for Alexandria—a small annoyance compared with the great discomfort and risk of going on and disembarking at Ismailia.

Nothing can be more inconvenient than the Canal route as at present organized. By it the patient is probably kept up all night expecting to have to disembark at any time from midnight to morn, thus risking chills from the cold night air, and loss of all sleep, with a long, uncomfortable, and uncertain start for Cairo by rail to follow.

To add to the discomfort, there is very inferior hotel accommodation and poor food obtainable at Ismailia, while there are only two so-called fast trains a day, leaving at 1.15 p.m. and 6.30 p.m., so that the invalid has many weary hours to remain there, after a very broken night's rest on board in the Canal, if he has been fortunate enough to get any sleep at all.* .

Alexandria, on the contrary, is a port that is always entered in daylight. It has all the advantages of a big town—good hotels, &c , and a fast service of trains to Cairo, which arrive there in time for lunch or dinner.

SHORT SEA. For those who prefer a short sea passage of three or five days—*via* Naples or Brindisi are the best routes to take. In this case the land journey is the most trying.

---

* It is thought that as soon as the railway from Port Said to Cairo *via* Ismailia, is in proper working order, some of these disadvantages will be done away with.

CAUTIONS TO BE OBSERVED ON THE LAND JOURNEY. It is a mistake for invalids to undertake the whole distance without a break somewhere *en route*.* Travelling by train is in itself a rapid change of climate, and is to most people exciting—the system is heated, and if any inflammatory mischief is present, it will probably be aggravated. Care should be taken to combat this state before starting by a strict attention to the state of the bowels, and by as careful a dietary as possible, both as to quantity and quality, during the journey, and to rest for a while, should it appear necessary *en route*. Much injury thus often arises from a want of attention to these details, and accounts for the more serious condition of some patients on their arrival, causing surprise to friends that such a case should have been sent away from home, whilst a little forethought and prudent and timely advice and treatment might have prevented it. For the sake of illustration let me cite a case as it occurred :—

DANGER OF OVER-FATIGUE AND EXCITEMENT. A. B., suffering from diabetes, was recommended to winter in Egypt, no particular place being specified. He arrived in the beginning of November, having left London only the week previously. When he left home the temperature was about 45°, on arrival in Cairo it was nearer 85°. Notwithstanding the fatigue and excitement of this rapid journey, and the great change of temperature and general surroundings

---

* Paris and Turin are the most convenient places to stop at between London and Brindisi.

to which he was in this brief period subjected, he spent the first week in Cairo in active sightseeing—finishing up with the ascent of the Great Pyramid. The same night he was attacked with severe diarrhœa, and died the next day from diabetic coma. How little, it thus appears, did this patient, who was sent out for the benefit of his health, know how to treat himself, and how totally he, in his ignorance, disregarded the very object of his journey, the sad sequel shows. Had he only been forewarned, and received some timely advice and caution, a valuable life would not thus have been sacrificed.

I could multiply *ad infinitum* cases showing equal stupidity, not perhaps ending fatally, but so aggravating the condition of those affected that any benefit likely to be derived from the change was greatly retarded, if not altogether lost. Physicians at home should not cease to impress on their patients the necessity for rest on the journey, and the importance of avoiding over fatigue and excitement on their arrival. They should travel only such distances each day as their strength will allow. Thus will another of the disadvantages as to distance from England disappear, the patient arriving at the end of his journey in a better state of health than when he left home, instead of suffering from evils the injurious effects of which are felt throughout the whole winter.

CHOICE OF WINTER QUARTERS. Invalids should, if possible, make up their minds before arriving in Egypt, where they intend to spend the winter whether in the neighbourhood of Cairo, or up the

Nile at Luxor or Assouan. If the former, they have
the choice of Mena House, or Helouan. Rooms
should be chosen or engaged beforehand, so that
invalids have not the trouble of doing so after the
fatigue of a troublesome journey. In most cases it
is not possible, and it is always inad-
visable, for invalids to proceed to Cairo
by the morning express (which leaves
Alexandria at 9.30 a.m., and arrives
at Cairo about 12.30 p.m.) *on the same day* that
the steamer arrives in port. They are, therefore,
strongly recommended, in any case, to spend the
day and night at Abbat's, or the Khedivial hotel,
in Alexandria, and not to come on by the afternoon
express, which does not arrive till late in the evening
in Cairo. Leaving by the morning express the next
day, much refreshed, and quite recovered from the
fatigue and effects of the sea voyage, and in a better
frame of mind to enjoy the novel and picturesque
sights to be seen on the railway journey to Cairo,
they arrive in time for lunch. Here they can take up
their quarters, if thought desirable—or can either
proceed to Helouan, a journey of about 40 minutes,
with an hourly service ; or drive to Mena, well provided
with wraps, starting not later than 3 p.m., so as to
arrive before sunset at their destination, having taken
the precaution of telegraphing to "Mena House,
Cairo," before leaving Alexandria, for a carriage to
meet them and their luggage at the station. These
may seem small details, but they are of great importance to health and comfort. Should the invalid,
however, have decided on going up the Nile, he should

START FOR CAIRO DAY FOLLOWING ARRIVAL IN ALEXANDRIA.

do so by the first opportunity, December and January being the best months there. Many, through ignorance, reverse this order, going up the river in February and March, thereby losing the most favourable periods of the season at each place.*

Invalids, therefore, on arriving in Egypt, have five places to choose from, *i.e.*,

HEALTH RESORTS.

1. Cairo itself.
2. Helouan ⎫ both near Cairo ;
3. Mena House ⎭
4. Luxor ⎫ both up the Nile.
5. Assouan ⎭

And as a place for sojourn in the spring, Ramleh may be mentioned.

CAIRO.

Cairo. "The most interesting of all places is, as yet, unhygienic, and full of dangerous dissipation to the invalid, but full of attractions to the healthy tourist" (Hermann Weber). Visitors are referred for information to the various published guide books.

HELOUAN.

Helouan is a suburb of Cairo, distant about 12 miles. It possesses sulphur baths somewhat similar to those at Aix-les-Bains. " It is entirely under the influence of the desert, and it is a most useful place to invalids suffering from rheumatism and early consumption, but it is some-

---

* The attention of invalids is drawn to the fact, that travellers by Messrs. T. Cook and Son's tickets and coupons are met on board the P. and O. steamers at the port of disembarkation by their agents ; and by them luggage is seen through the customs, and forwarded to its destination without any trouble or fatigue on the owner's part.

what monotonous to those accustomed to social excitement " (Hermann Weber).

MENA HOUSE.   *Mena House* has all the advantages of an English country house, with every luxury and home comfort.   It lies on the edge of the desert, at the foot of the Great Pyramid of Gizeh, surrounded by the purest desert air, free from the temptations and inconveniences of a big town, while yet within easy reach of Cairo.   It is far enough away at the same time from the city to enable the invalid to resist the opportunities of undoing the good effects of change of climate by sightseeing, over-fatigue, late hours, &c., such as exist in the town itself.   This, to some classes of health-seekers, may seem a drawback, but invalids must sacrifice for a short time their inclinations and pleasures, if they are to get the benefit they desire, and may expect from a winter in Egypt.

MEDICAL OPINIONS OF MENA.   Various notices have from time to time appeared in the medical journals descriptive of Mena, from which I will now give a few extracts :—

(a) Dr. Hermann Weber says :—" Close to the Great Pyramid of Gizeh is an excellently-arranged hotel, which offers amusement of varied kind to the healthy as well as to the invalid.   It lies at the edge of the desert, and the invalid may spend much of his time in the desert itself, and enjoy its invigorating air from morning till night."

(b) Dr. Burdon Sanderson, in the *Practitioner* for 1890, vol. I., says :—" If you want above all *rest* of

body and mind, absolute immunity from cold winds and inclement weather, and unlimited sunshine, you will find what you want in the valley of the Nile. Make your home for the former at the Pyramids (Mena); for the latter on a dahabeah; or, if that is unattainable, on a Postal steamer, spending as few nights as possible in hotels"; and again, he says, "as regards Cairo, the advice to give them (patients), is, to avoid living in it. There is now no longer any difficulty in doing this, and that, without sacrificing the pleasures and advantages of exploring it thoroughly. Close to the Pyramids of Gizeh, an hour and a half's distance from Cairo, a hotel (Mena) has been built on a slope leading up to the rocky plateau on which these wonders of the world stand. The air is that of the desert, the comforts enjoyed by guests is that of a first-class hotel, with the advantages that under the advice of Dr. Sandwith, the arrangements have been made with special reference to the needs of invalids."

(c) Dr. Sandwith, in the *Practitioner*, vol. II., for 1890, says :—" Favourable mention has already been made in the *Practitioner* of a new hotel built at the foot of the Pyramid, with a special view to provide the guest with English home requirements. The water for all purposes is taken from a reservoir, supplied by wells in the desert, some 50 feet deep, and even before

ANALYSIS OF WATER AT MENA HOUSE. being filtered is remarkably pure. The following is an accurate analysis in grammes per litre :—

Free ammonia	.000026.
Carbonate of calcium	.1107.
Carbonate of magnesium	.0330.
Chloride of do.	.0150.
Chloride of sodium	.0174.
Sulphate of do.	.0337.
Nitrate of do.	.0134.
Silicate of potassium	.0144.
Silica	.0255.
Oxide of iron and alumina	.0009.
Organic matter	.0040.

Again, he says in his work, "Egypt as a Winter Resort" :—"Those who do not know the Cairo of to-day will be most surprised to hear of the existence of a first-class hotel at the foot of the Pyramid. The air is so pure and dry that it cannot be praised too highly. It is invaluable to those who do not want the fatigue and expense of a voyage up the Nile." *

EXPENSE OF THE TRIP. As regards the next consideration, the Expense of the trip, much may be done by forethought and care to minimise this drawback. A first class return ticket, available for four months, may be obtained by the P. & O. for the following prices :—

---

* Cost of trip up the Nile to Assouan and back to Cairo :—
By Messrs. T. Cook and Son's Tourist boats, £50 to £60 (return) ;
By   do.   Post boats, £21 to £25 (return) ;
By   do.   Dahabeah, from £50 to £400
a month, according to the size of the boat, number of passengers, and style of accommodation required. For further particulars, see Messrs. T. Cook and Son's programme of International tickets to Egypt.

1. London to Alexandria, and back from Port Said to London £33 0 0

2. London to Alexandria, *via* Paris, Turin, and Brindisi, and back the same route, including railway fare. £42 8 6

Sleeping car £4 12 0 extra.

3. London by sea to Naples—thence to Alexandria, and back to Naples only £28 0 0

4. London, by rail *via* Naples, to Alexandria ; and back the same way, including railway fare £42 8 6

Invalids who wish to remain in Egypt longer than four months have a concession of 20% on returning off the ordinary first class single fare.*

There is really little or no difficulty in obtaining accommodation on the return journey at the end of the season, if a little forethought is exercised by the traveller in applying for a berth. I am informed, on the best authority, that the P. & O. Company have sometimes as many as thirteen steamers passing through the Canal homewards each month, besides the regular boats, which leave Alexandria for Brindisi, or Naples, every week or ten days, during the season ; so that there are always ample opportunities of return. During the last season (1893-4) there has not been a P. & O. steamer passing the Canal that has not had available accommodation on leaving Egypt.

---

* For further information, see P. & O. Handbook of Information.

COST OF LIVING IN CAIRO OR MENA.
At any of the hotels in Cairo and at Mena, board and lodging can be obtained for 16s. a day, or 14s. 6d. by the month ; this, at Mena, is inclusive, excepting only wines and washing. Taking the whole season's expenses through, 20s. to 30s. a day should be sufficient for everything, passage out and home included, and the keep of a horse during the winter. Visitors are recommended, if staying at Mena, to buy their own horse, and to take out a bridle and saddle with them, on which, if they have been used before, no duty is levied at Alexandria.

VICISSITUDES OF THE CLIMATE OF EGYPT.
The risks and discomforts to which all new comers are exposed, from a want of knowledge of the vicissitudes of the climate, and of the comparatively cold winds that blow more or less in December and January, are at times trying, but easily avoidable. They are more or less felt around Cairo, and are especially to be guarded against by those making the Nile trip. "To be forewarned is to be forearmed." Nearly all climates are variable, none more so than England ; but whereas in the latter the changes are frequent and limited, in Egypt they are sudden and extensive.

The diurnal temperature of Egypt is very uniform, but the sudden fall at sunset of several degrees, reaching its climax at about 4 a.m., is felt by invalids whose sensitiveness to cold is at all times marked, if they are foolish enough to expose themselves to it. It is a well-known fact that, even by the robust, the sensibility to cold is increased as the south is approached. All invalids, therefore, should go in-

doors an hour before sunset, and should not venture out till two hours after sunrise. Again, nothing is
GREAT DIFFERENCE IN TEMPERATURE BETWEEN SUNSHINE AND SHADE.
more noticeable than the great difference there is between sunshine and shade. This is very marked when driving along the roads about Cairo, and also in going to Mena from Cairo, under the lovely avenue of "Lebbek trees,"* which line the carriage drive the whole way ; and also in the houses and passages of the hotels in Cairo, where the temperature is often
HOW TO AVOID ILL-EFFECTS.
below that of the open air. This disadvantage is, however, easily avoided by invalids wearing as warm clothing in Egypt as
WARM WOOLLEN CLOTHING NECESSARY.
they do in the autumn or winter at home, the air being so dry that any oppressiveness from woollen clothing is not felt there ; also by their carrying always a light coat, or wrap, and a silk handkerchief for the neck, to be put on when going from sunshine into the shade ; while in the house, after a walk, they should not remove their
CUMMERBUNDS TO BE WORN BY ALL.
overcoats at once. Cummerbunds, or a roll of fine flannel round the abdomen, should be worn by all as a preventive of diarrhœa, &c., arising from chills, and a heavy or fur-lined coat should always be used when driving. All rooms, facing the north, should be provided with fireplaces, and a fire kept burning in December and January, when the weather is cold or
FIRE IN BEDROOM.
unsettled. I am informed that this winter (1894) the passages and large halls at Mena are to be heated up to a uniform temperature. In

---

* Albizzia Lebbek.

addition almost every bedroom has a fireplace, and the sitting-rooms have large open fires burning all through the winter, which is not the case in any of the hotels in Cairo.

DANGERS ARISING FROM CHILLS. Want of attention to these points may lead to chills, with their possible consequences, such as diarrhœa, dysentery, or pneumonia, or an aggravation of the symptoms of their complaint, or to a fresh access of inflammation in a quiescent chronic condition of lung disease. Care is also necessary at times in ladies, to avoid the possible chance of a chill—a case having come to my knowledge last winter where severe local peritonitis followed exposure to cold in this way after a ride.

DIRECT SUN-RAYS TO BE GUARDED AGAINST. The direct rays of the sun, if not tempered by the use of an umbrella, or suitable head-protection, or smoked spectacles, more especially in March and April, is often injurious, leading to congestions, headaches and feverishness ; the latter, especially in children with a strumous tendency. I have so often seen invalids sit or lie in the direct rays of the sun, while at the same time a cold wind was blowing over them, that I am induced to lay stress on the folly and THEIR ILL-EFFECTS. possible danger of this. Clarke, on "Climate," on this point says :—" One of the most exciting things to a sensitive invalid is exposure to a powerful sun " ; and, again, " persons with the slightest disposition to inflammation of the throat, trachea, or lungs, should avoid exposure to cold, or high winds, or a powerful sun, or still more to alternations of these."

THE NILE VOYAGE. Now it is especially to these conditions that the invalid is exposed on going up and coming down the Nile, the days being warm, the wind keen, while the cold after sunset is intense ; the warmest clothing and wraps are therefore necessary on the voyage. Draughts, which are

PRECAUTIONS NECESSARY TO BE ADOPTED ON THE BOAT. unavoidable, should, as far as possible, be guarded against, even if necessary by the invalid remaining for the most of the time in the saloon or in his cabin, and on no account should he go on deck after sunset. Over-fatigue in any form, and long donkey rides to tombs and other distant places of interest, should be scrupulously declined by the consumptive, labouring more or less as they do under physical debility. Such should not attempt to take part in the amuse-ments and occupations of the strong, but cheerfully acquiesce in their enforced idleness, for, by doing so, they very materially advance their chances of ultimate recovery.

MESSRS. T. COOK & SON'S NILE TOURIST BOATS. The tour made by the regular tourist boat of Messrs. T. Cook and Son, each of which carries an experienced physician, and is a floating palace of splendour and luxury, is well suited to the robust pleasure-seeker, but is not the best way of reaching

POST-BOATS. Luxor for the invalid. The post-boat, being more direct, is for him by far the

best, if he is unable to afford the expense of a
DAHABEAHS.   dahabeah on the Nile for the winter.

Dr. Hermann Weber, writing to me on this subject,
DR.   says :—" The travelling on the Nile
HERMANN WEBER'S
OPINION.   steamers is most enjoyable to
healthy persons, owing to the constant change of scene,
the life of the natives, and the excursions ; but
it is not well adapted to invalids, owing to
frequent draughts, great differences in temperature between day and night and sun and
shade.   I have often seen throat affections, catarrhs,
and rheumatism during the journeys up and down
the Nile.   The dahabeah, with its slower movement,
is rather better adapted to invalids."   The same
authority adds :—

LUXOR.   " *Luxor*, with its temples and good hotels,
           is a delightful health-resort "; and

ASSOUAN.   " *Assouan*, near the first cataract, has
           still greater advantages, especially to
rheumatic and consumptive persons, owing to the
greater dryness there of the air."

THE KHAMSEEN.   The hot wind, or Khamseen, com-
                mences in February, and blows for a
day or two at a time, but only very occasionally,
till the middle of April.   It has a depressing effect
on some, while it is agreeable and invigorating to
others.   During its continuance the air is devoid of
all moisture, and is more or less charged with
electricity, while it is at the same time full of small,
minute particles of sand in a state of suspension,

ITS ILL-EFFECTS causing irritation of the eyes and throat. It has, however, a more irritating effect on the temper than an injurious one on the health. It is less disagreeable to many than the colder winds of ITS GOOD EFFECTS. December and January, and in cases of phthisis, with cavities, it has a positive drying up and healing influence. Its good effects also in rheumatism, and some cases of asthma, are HOW TO OBVIATE ITS DISCOMFORTS. marked. Its discomforts are entirely obviated by the invalid remaining in-doors till it has blown itself out, which it generally does in about two days.

There are no insect-pests at Mena. Mosquitoes are INSECT-PESTS. absent, owing to the want of water for them to breed in. Flies are trouble-some only in March and April.

EARLY DEPAR-TURE IN THE SPRING NOT ADVISABLE. As a rule invalids leave Egypt too soon in the spring, and undo in many cases the good effects of their winter sojourn by encountering the cold, variable weather of the spring in Europe. Let me warn them against this, and, in place of hurrying off as soon as the first khamseen blows, to remain quietly in Egypt till the end of April. If they find the neigh-bourhood of Cairo too hot and enervating, there is RAMLEH. *Ramleh*, on the sea coast, near Alexandria to go to, where excellent hotel accommo-dation can now be obtained, and where they will run no risks of encountering the chills of an early spring ALEXANDRIA. "The neighbourhood of Alexandria, owing to the nearness of the sea, has a more uniform temperature, and has advantages in autumn, spring, and summer." (Hermann Weber.)

NURSING. Every facility exists in Cairo, Mena, and Luxor for obtaining medical comforts and good nursing. On this score there is little left to be desired. Invalids, however, who require constant attention, are strongly recommended to bring with them their own nurse or valet.

DR. BENTLEY'S address is *in Summer*, 64, HARLEY ST., W., and *in Winter*, CAIRO.

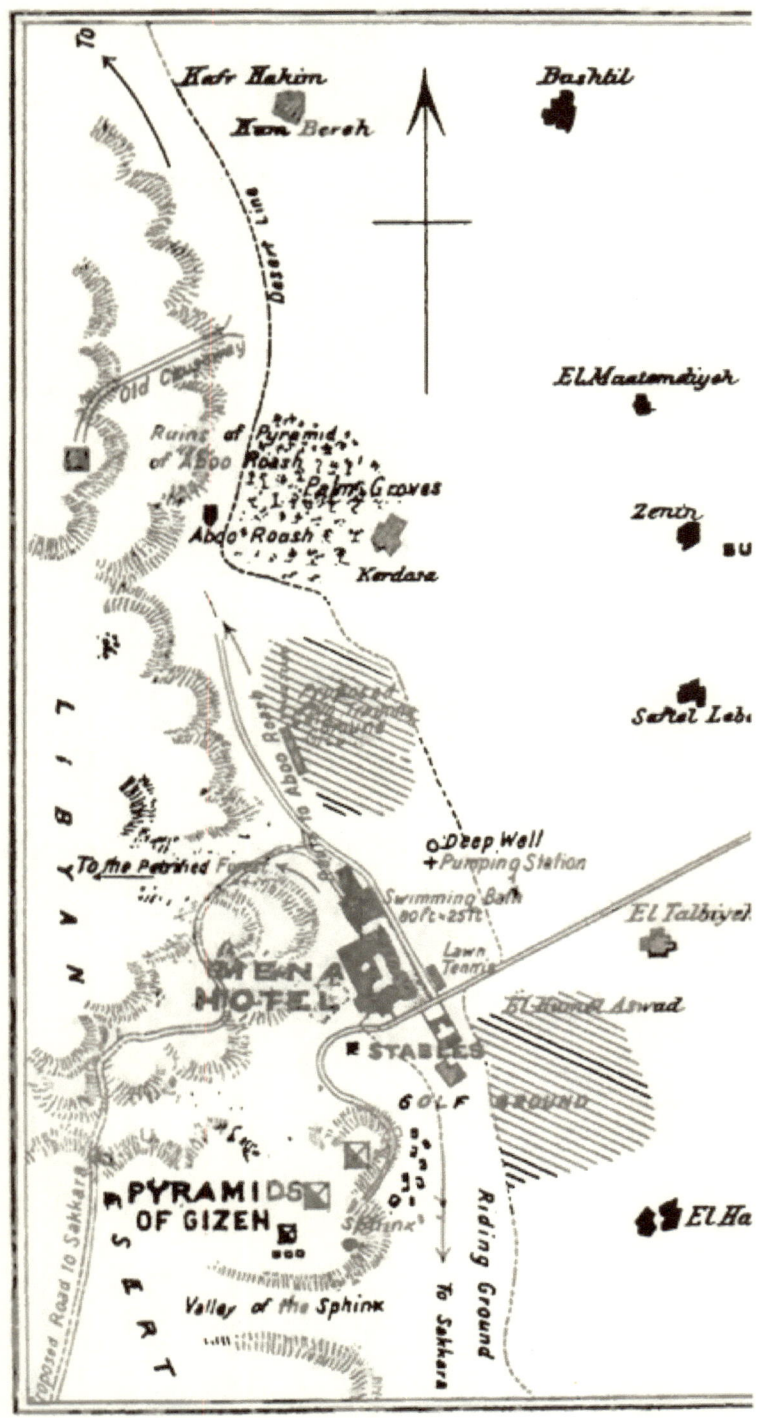

OLD
CAIRO

3TA

GEBEL
MOKATTAM 630

the more important varieties of the disease.........Neurologists would do well to study Dr. Bentley's cases.......Besides these there are many other interesting points in this work we should like to notice, did space permit.......We have little doubt this work will be extensively read and much appreciated, especially by practitioners in the tropics, and that it will act as a powerful stimulus in leading others to endeavour to extend our knowledge of the very interesting and important subject of which it treats "—*British Medical Journal*, February 10, 1894.

"To the planter, the miner, the colonist, and the ruler in our tropical dependencies, the subject of Beri-beri is only second in practical importance to malaria and, perhaps, cholera. Such being the case, any important contribution to our knowledge of the disease can only be welcome. We can safely say that Dr. Bentley's work is one of the most valuable contributions to our knowledge of the subject which of late years has seen the light.........The systematic records of pulse, temperature, urine, and so forth, attached to each case, are of much value, and effectually dispose of more than one of the many crude theories which have been advanced about this disease......... There are many other points we would like to mention, but those which we have briefly alluded to will show our readers that there is much of novelty and interest in this volume.........These are small matters in comparison with the genuine merits of this work, which we trust will serve to direct the attention of the profession to a disease of the highest importance, hitherto too much neglected."—*The Practitioner*, Vol. li., No. 6.

"This treatise well deserved the gold medal which it obtained when presented as a thesis for the M.D. degree in 1889. Beri-beri is a disease concerning which true etiology and pathology presents many points of difficulty, and Dr. Bentley has been fortunate in obtaining a thorough acquaintance with it, and has given us a detailed clinical account of fifty-two cases, and the post-mortem results seen in nineteen. The ten illustrations are admirable, and give a vivid picture of the various phases of the disease.........The book will be invaluable for those practising in the various regions where the disease is indigenous."—*Edinburgh Medical Journal*, January 7, 1894.

"This book is a classical contribution to the study of Beri-Beri."— *Medical Press*, September. 1894.

(Young J. Pentland, Publishers, Edinburgh and London, 1893.)

Also by Rev. C. G. GRIFFINHOOFE, M.A.

Small post 8vo, cloth boards, 1s.,

SPOKES IN THE WHEEL OF LIFE :

Addresses to Young Men.

" This is a volume of earnest and practical addresses delivered at St. Andrew's, Wells Street. They are pointed and incisive, and contain much excellent advice on matters touching a young man's life and worldly success, as well as counsel of a more directly religious character. Manysidedness is a useful chapter. The connection between Sabbath-keeping and health of mind and body is forcibly set forth, and we only wish all the youths of our acquaintance would take to heart the warnings against unpunctuality."—*Record.*

SOCIETY FOR PROMOTING CHRISTIAN KNOWLEDGE,
NORTHUMBERLAND AVENUE, S.W.

Small Post 8vo, 6d.,

EGYPT IN THE BIBLE,

A Sermon preached at Mena House, Pyramids,

APRIL 23rd, 1893.

TEMPLE & Co., 69, WELLS STREET, W.

Printed at the Operative Jewish Converts' Institution, Palestine Place,
Cambridge Heath, London, E.

.

www.ingramcontent.com/pod-product-compliance
Lightning Source LLC
Chambersburg PA
CBHW030554040726
47497CB00008B/2723